"I think we should get married,"

she said hesitantly.

"Why would you want to marry me, Shelley?"

"It's the most logical thing to do, given the circumstances. I guess what I'm talking about is a marriage of convenience. A mutually beneficial arrangement. If we got married, you could have everything you want. This house, and as quickly as possible, your kids. I would get a place to stay."

He reached for her hand and enfolded it in both of his. Offering as much as she could give, she was responding to both their needs. What's more, he knew marriage was probably the only way he could keep her in his life right now.

He was good for her. He could see that. She'd said as much. But could he give her a year and then let her walk away? He'd find out soon enough.

"Then I guess we're engaged."

Dear Reader,

Autumn inspires visions of the great outdoors, but Special Edition lures you back inside with six vibrant romances!

Many of the top-selling mainstream authors today launched their careers writing series romance. Some special authors have achieved remarkable success in the mainstream with both hardcovers and paperbacks, yet continue to support the genre and the readers they love. *New York Times* bestselling author Nora Roberts is just such an author, and this month we're delighted to bring you *The Winning Hand,* the eighth book in her popular series THE MACGREGORS.

In *Father-to-Be* by Laurie Paige, October's tender THAT'S MY BABY! title, an impulsive night of passion changes a rugged rancher's life forever. And if you enjoy sweeping medical dramas, we prescribe *From House Calls to Husband* by Christine Flynn, part of PRESCRIPTION: MARRIAGE. This riveting new series by three Silhouette authors highlights nurses who vow never to marry a doctor. Look for the second installment of the series next month.

Silhouette's new five-book cross-line continuity series, FOLLOW THAT BABY, introduces the Wentworth oil tycoon family and their search for a missing heir. The series begins in Special Edition this month with *The Rancher and the Amnesiac Bride* by Joan Elliott Pickart, then crosses into Romance (11/98), Desire (12/98), Yours Truly (1/99) and concludes in Intimate Moments (2/99).

Also, check out *Partners in Marriage* by Allison Hayes, in which a vulnerable schoolteacher invades a Lakota man's house—and his heart! Finally, October's WOMAN TO WATCH is talented newcomer Jean Brashear, who unfolds a provocative tale of revenge—and romance—in *The Bodyguard's Bride.*

I hope you enjoy all of the stories this month!

Sincerely,

Karen Taylor Richman
Senior Editor

Please address questions and book requests to:
Silhouette Reader Service
U.S.: 3010 Walden Ave., P.O. Box 1325, Buffalo, NY 14269
Canadian: P.O. Box 609, Fort Erie, Ont. L2A 5X3

ALLISON HAYES

PARTNERS IN MARRIAGE

Silhouette® F HAY

SPECIAL EDITION®

Published by Silhouette Books
America's Publisher of Contemporary Romance

For my grandparents, E. C. and Janice Coddington,
South Dakota educators par excellence.

 SILHOUETTE BOOKS

ISBN 0-373-24205-0

PARTNERS IN MARRIAGE

Books by Allison Hayes

Silhouette Special Edition

Marry Me, Now! #1032
Partners in Marriage #1205

ALLISON HAYES

was born in Deadwood, South Dakota, and keeps returning to the state, both in person and through the imaginary settings of her books. A student of Lakota history and culture, she taught at a South Dakota tribal college and has never worked with such fine students, before or since. The author of both historical and category romance novels, Allison has a Ph.D. in language and literacy education and currently teaches at the University of California at Berkeley.

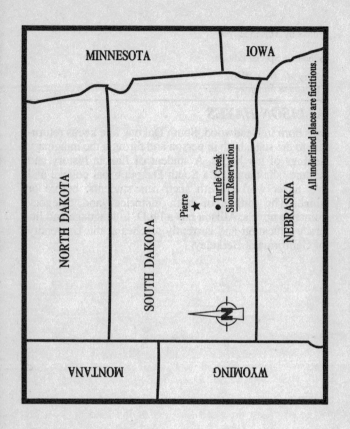

MINNESOTA

IOWA

NORTH DAKOTA

SOUTH DAKOTA

NEBRASKA

MONTANA

WYOMING

Pierre ★

● Turtle Creek
  Sioux Reservation

N

All underlined places are fictitious.

Chapter One

There was one house left to rent in the county, and Shelley Mathews was going to have it if she had to crawl through the rocky March County gumbo on her hands and knees to get it.

"Mr. Heber?" She caught up with her prospective landlord, Melvin Heber, in front of the post office. Mail in hand, he was reaching for the door of his baby blue pickup.

The old man adjusted the bill of his feed cap—it advertised the March-Whitlock Electrical Co-op—and squinted suspiciously at her.

Shelley plastered on the brightest smile she could muster. "I'm Shelley Mathews. I'll be teaching at the high school this year, and I'm looking for a house to rent."

"What's that?" Mr. Heber leaned closer and turned his left ear toward her.

"I'm a new teacher at the high school," she said

loudly, holding the determined smile. "Joe Bernard from the café told me you have a house for rent near town."

"Oh!" He folded his mail under one arm. "You looking for a place to live?"

"Yes. I've been looking for a week. I haven't found anything."

"Not many places around here. Joe sent you, did you say?"

Trying not to let her desperation show, she nodded.

Mr. Heber bobbed his head. "I do have a nice little house west of town. Folks who had it left yesterday. Real close to town. Quiet."

As long as it had functional plumbing, she wanted it. "Can I see it?"

"Sure. I'm going out there now to check the furnace. Make sure it works good. You just follow me. You're a teacher, did you say?"

She was starting to feel more relaxed. "Yes. I'll be teaching tenth-grade history."

"Had lots of teachers as tenants," Mr. Heber said approvingly. "It's a good house. I raised my boys there. You married? Got a family?"

Shelley froze. After all these years, this simple question still hurt. "It's just me."

"What's that?" He leaned closer.

"I'm not married." She cringed at how loud her voice sounded on the quiet street.

Heber smiled for the first time. "Single women make good tenants. Usually keep the place up real good. That your car?" He pointed at the dusty compact car with California plates.

"Yes."

He opened the door of his truck and tossed the mail onto the seat. "Well, come on. It's not far."

Shelley got in her car and followed the big pickup onto the main street of Gilbert, South Dakota, population 1,038. Smack-dab in the middle of nowhere, Gilbert was part of the Turtle Creek Sioux Reservation. If there were any sights beyond the endless sky and rolling plains, Shelley hadn't been privileged to view them. The amenities consisted of a Taco Charley's, a couple of grocery stores, one small motel and two or three filling stations with convenience stores attached. At the western edge of town, Mr. Heber pulled onto the shoulder to negotiate the sharp right turn onto a gravel section road.

Across a mile or more of marshy pasture, Shelley could see a small house surrounded by large trees. From this distance, it looked much better than the dilapidated fifty-year-old trailer she'd seen yesterday, or the eight-by-ten room in a messy, crowded home she'd seen the day before. As bad as those had been, both had already been rented by the time Shelley got to them. As she looked at Mr. Heber's house, her spirits rose.

Gravel crunched under her tires as her car bounced up and down over a washboarded section of the road, and she thought about how far she was from home. She'd never been to South Dakota before. She'd applied for the job because her parents had insisted she make a life of her own again. Shelley had agreed and decided to make it as far from San Diego as she could and applied at remote schools around the world. Barely two weeks ago, after a phone interview with the principal, she'd been offered a job teaching tenth-grade history at March County High School. Four days later, she'd been on the road, and now she was in the midst of the new life everyone said she needed.

Her old life wasn't far from mind, though. Shelley wondered what Brad would have thought of Gilbert and this jouncy, dusty road. He would have wanted to know what was growing in that field to the right, and why the field to the left wasn't fenced. He would have teased her just enough to cheer her up when she wanted to cry because she couldn't find a place to live. Teacher housing was full and there were no houses, apartments or rooms for rent in the tiny reservation towns. The nearest off-reservation town, Arrowhead, Nebraska, was thirty-five miles away and not much better. In her old life, Brad would have known what to do. He wouldn't have let her think about going home. But Brad was gone, and as much as she wished it wasn't, Shelley knew this adventure was hers alone.

A mile down the little lane, they turned left. Half a mile farther, she trailed Mr. Heber into a long, rutted driveway that led back to the house and some outbuildings.

After turning off the air-conditioning, Shelley rolled down her window. It was mid-August, warm and still, and the air was sweet with the scent of grass and earth. She recognized the purple flowers of a late alfalfa crop in the field and admired the tiny butterflies dancing over them. Somewhere in the field, a blackbird trilled a hopeful song.

Shelley pulled into the parking area in front of a car shed and got out of the car. On closer inspection, the house was simple, an old-fashioned, one-story ranch house. There were no frills—not so much as a single window box. Though it had seemed neat and trim from a distance, Shelley now saw peeling white paint and an overgrown yard. The only flowers were the volunteer hollyhocks dotting the western half of the yard, their straight stalks of red and pink flowers reaching for the sky. A chicken-wire fence staked on old branches ran around the perimeter of the yard, and inside it marched a row of mature Siberian elms. They were big trees for the prairie, stalwart and protective, but full of dry, dead wood. Though run-down, the house held a forlorn charm that appealed to Shelley. It looked a bit like she felt—a little the worse for wear but functional.

A meadowlark called in the field, its voice strong and clear. Shelley imagined invitation in its song, and she decided she would like listening to the meadowlarks and blackbirds every morning. This little house, she thought, could make a good home.

A battered yellow pickup appeared on a dirt track that emerged from a dense windbreak west of the house, and the meadowlark's song was displaced by the bass throb of engine noise. The truck rocked unevenly over deep ruts as it approached and circled into the wide parking area. The driver, an Indian man, parked next to Mr. Heber's truck and turned off the engine. When he got out, a black-and-tan dog of indeterminate breed hopped down off the seat behind him.

Any lingering sense of well-being Shelley felt drained swiftly away. One glimpse of this man's set expression told her that whoever he was, he didn't want her here. His eyes were shuttered and his jaw clenched. She watched him shake hands with Mr. Heber, then nod curtly in her direction without meeting her gaze.

Mr. Heber greeted the younger man easily. "You been clearing out some of that dead wood back there?"

"I thought I'd get a head start on a woodpile." The man spoke with an accent Shelley was coming to recognize as typical for the area. The words were a little clipped, the cadence gentle.

Mr. Heber bobbed his head toward Shelley. "This is one of the new teachers at the high school."

"Shelley Mathews," she supplied, extending a hand.

The man glanced at her without a scrap of expression in his eyes, but he accepted her hand. "Blue Larson."

His hand was warm and callused, and he let go immediately. Shelley tried a smile and got no response.

"You're here for the house," he said.

There was challenge and something Shelley couldn't quite define in his statement.

"Yes. I've been looking for something since I arrived a week ago. This is the first place I've seen that hasn't been rented before I got to it."

A muscle ticked in Blue Larson's cheek as he looked at the house. Then he glanced down at the dog sitting at his feet and sighed. When the animal butted Blue's hand, he scratched the dog's ears absently. His gaze returned to the house.

Heber handed Shelley a key. "Go on in and take a look. See what you think."

Uncomfortable, Shelley was glad to leave the two men. Was Larson a hired man? He certainly wasn't pleased to meet her, whoever he was.

The concrete stairs that led up to the small porch were a little too high and not quite level, but they were sturdy. The door opened into a small entryway. There was a small living room with one bedroom off it on the east side of the house, a huge kitchen and dining room in the middle and two more small bedrooms and a bath on the west side. The bedrooms were small. The kitchen counters were bloodred, and the wallpaper was covered with gold steamboats, locomotives and stagecoaches, all lurching their way through a thick coating of grease. The bathroom walls looked like laminated pink cardboard, and the dark, cobwebby basement could have served as the set for a horror movie, but the toilet flushed and the shower worked.

The house was full of light with many windows and high ceilings. With a good cleaning and fresh paint, it would be pleasant. It would be home. Shelley felt a tremendous sense of relief.

Shelley had her hand on the outside door, on her way to tell Mr. Heber she'd take the house, when Blue Larson's voice stopped her.

"I thought we had a deal." His voice was tight.

"Well, you haven't moved in yet, and this girl needs a place. You've been staying at your cousin's place. Stay a while longer. In a few months some place else will open up."

"I can't stay at my cousin's. Her daughter's expecting a baby in two weeks, and they need the space. You already told me I could have this house."

"You don't have anything in writing," Heber countered.

"You've never rented this house with a written lease, and you told me I could have it."

"The girl needs it more."

Shelley pushed open the screen door. Both men looked at her, but it was Blue Larson's dark gaze she met.

"I'm sorry," she said carefully, trying to hide both her embarrassment and disappointment. "I didn't realize the house had been rented. I was so excited to see it, I didn't think that you might have already spoken with Mr. Heber." She wiped her hands across the seat of her shorts, unsure what to do. She looked back at the house, then shook her head. "I guess I'll be going."

"Now, wait a minute." Mr. Heber blocked her exit. "Didn't you like the house?"

"Yes, of course I liked it. But you've already rented it. I wish you'd told me."

"I can rent my property to anyone I choose," Heber declared. "The house is yours if you want it."

"I can't take it now." Shelley was aware that there was something at issue here that she couldn't quite pin down. "Mr. Larson, I hope you enjoy the house." She took a step toward the car.

"I can't rent it to him, anyway. You might as well take it," Heber insisted.

Shelley stopped. "Why can't you rent it to Mr. Larson?"

"I need a tenant who's got a full-time, reliable job. I have to protect my investment."

Shelley looked at Blue, noticing for the first time the red T-shirt he wore. It bore the emblem of the local tribal college. His hair was long in back, neatly tied. It startled her to realize that he was also a very handsome man. He wasn't tall, he wasn't terribly young, but he had an athletic grace and a clear, direct countenance. If appearances could be taken as any gauge of character, Blue Larson looked reliable.

"You don't have a job?" she asked him.

Larson's voice was even more clipped than it had been. "I'm in my senior year at the college. I work part-time in the computer center, and I coach track at the high school."

"I'll rent to the teacher," Mr. Heber said.

"Why not to him?" Shelley asked, pointing to Blue.

Blue answered her question before Heber could. "Because you're white."

Of course. The undercurrent she sensed had not been an undercurrent at all, but an ugly flood. She wasn't used to such blatant discrimination.

An unpleasant silence stretched between the three of them.

Mr. Heber was the one to break it. "It's illegal to discriminate against tenants on the basis of race," he said sanctimoniously. "She has a better income. Better credit, most likely."

Both Shelley and Blue eyed the old man with distaste. Shelley tried to think what to do. She didn't want to take the house under these circumstances, but there really weren't any other options. She couldn't afford to stay at the motel forever, and she doubted Heber would rent to Blue Larson now, no matter what she did. This house would have been perfect, even if it was a little bigger than she needed.

Bigger, she thought. With three bedrooms, two on one side of the house, one on the other. I wonder if he's single?

He wasn't wearing a ring.

The obvious thing would be to share the house. There was plenty of room. It would be strange to share with a man she didn't know, but it was the most practical solution to their problem. Since he coached at the high school, she would ask the principal about him, but intuition told her he was a decent person.

She wanted to talk to him alone for a few minutes.

"Mr. Heber, would you mind if I stayed out here awhile to make up my mind?"

That seemed to satisfy the old man. He bobbed his head and resettled the feed cap. "Don't see why not. I'll just go check out that furnace. Make sure there's a clean filter in it. You can find me at my house in town when you decide what to do. It's the gray one next to the Methodist church. This little house here is a good one. It's a real good house for a single woman."

Blue Larson whistled to his dog, who was nosing around along the fence line, and turned to go.

"Please wait," Shelley said softly so Heber wouldn't hear. "Until Mr. Heber goes. Please."

Blue cast her an assessing look, then walked back to his truck. The dog looked up once, but went on investigating. Blue set to rummaging in the bed of his pickup.

A few minutes later, the dust from Mr. Heber's departure hung like a curtain strung on an invisible cord above the road. Shelley leaned back against the high edge of the porch and watched his truck disappear from view. As the dust drifted slowly toward them, Blue crossed the yard to stand before her.

He was certainly handsome, she thought, with even bones, slanting eyebrows and a wide mouth that looked like it might have some wonderful smiles lurking behind the scowl he wore now. Shelley realized she hadn't looked this closely at a man in a very long time. Goodness, she thought, what a time to start.

She decided to dispense with small talk and get straight to the point.

"Do you have a family?" she asked.

"I've got two kids. They live with their mom in Wyoming. I was hoping to have them stay with me more often."

The three-bedroom house with so much space around it would have been perfect for a man with two children.

"So you live alone?"

"Yes."

Shelley looked him in the eye. "I've looked everywhere within a forty-mile radius of the high school. I can't find another place to live, and I've signed a contract with the school, so I can't leave."

Blue looked past her to the house. "There isn't anyplace else. The school district hired more teachers than they have housing for this year, and the hospital in Rosebud got a windfall from Washington for more doctors. The college hired more people, too, and housing's always short here. It's been three years since the tribe got an increase in housing money. Lots of families are crammed together." Blue paused. "But that isn't your problem. The house is yours. You heard the man."

"I need the house," Shelley repeated. "I'm going to take it, much as I'd like to throw it back in that man's face. But I'm only one person."

Blue's eyes narrowed.

"There are three bedrooms."

"Yeah," he agreed quietly. "There are."

"I could use a roommate. I've never lived alone and I don't know anyone in the area." She tried to sound positive. "I enjoy having someone to talk to."

Blue's lips twitched in a movement that wasn't a smile. Then he leaned one foot against the porch step and hooked a thumb into a belt loop. "You haven't been here very long to be taking up with an Indian buck."

Shelley stared at him a moment. "That's not what I meant."

His laugh wasn't nice.

She stayed calm. He was angry. She understood that. "I meant a roommate, not a lover. We both need a place to live. There's room for two single adults here. It's a logical solution. It isn't perfect, but it would give us both a place to live."

Blue's tone was rigid. "I don't want to live here on your charity."

"I'm not offering you charity. I would expect you to pay half of the rent and utilities."

He made a rude noise.

She should give up. Not quite understanding why, she didn't.

"I don't see what's so unusual about two people sharing a house. It's a practical move."

"Ms. Mathews, it took me months to convince Heber to rent me this place. You saw him today. One pretty white woman shows up looking for a house, saying please with big eyes and a sad smile, and that's it. I'm out of the picture. Heber doesn't like Indians. He never wanted to rent to me, but he couldn't think of a safe excuse not to. I chased off everyone in the next ten counties who so much as hinted that they were interested in this place. It wasn't easy, but I got Heber to agree to let me have it."

His voice rose with his anger, but he didn't frighten Shelley. She knew what it felt like to have parts of your life taken away, important parts, vital parts. She listened calmly.

"This place is everything I ever wanted," he continued. "There's enough room for my kids to stay with me. There's a barn and a corral where I can keep a few horses. There's room for a garden, fields to walk across at dusk, a good pasture, and I'm close to town and the college. I study hard, I work hard and I want my own place. I can't buy it yet, but Heber is old. He'll sell in a few years. If he sees me take care of things, he might sell to me, even though I'm an Indian." He paused. "How long will you be here?"

"I don't know."

"Most teachers come here for a year, maybe two. Not very many of them stay. Will you?"

"I don't know."

He snorted derisively. "Why did you come here?

ALLISON HAYES   19

Think you're going to improve the plight of the poor Indians?''

It was Shelley's turn to laugh.

Blue Larson hadn't felt this helpless and just plain cussing mad since his marriage had fallen apart five years ago. He'd been so close to getting the house he'd had his eye on for four years, and this cool, distant woman waltzed in and took it from him. Now she had the gall to laugh at him when all he'd done was point out what he was pretty sure was the truth.

Damn it, the woman was laughing hard. He waited for her to stop.

"That comment is generally taken as an insult," he said.

"I gathered as much. I'm sorry. I wasn't laughing at you. More at myself."

Her eyes went sad again, though she smiled.

He couldn't help the question. "Why is that?"

She tilted her head a little. "I came out here to get as far away from San Diego as I could. I applied for jobs in Borneo, Alaska, even Greenland. Until I talked to the principal two weeks ago, I didn't know March County High School was anywhere near an Indian reservation. I just thought it would be rural America. It was a change. That was all I was looking for. I wasn't prepared for people with a *plight*."

Blue didn't know what to say. Shelley Mathews was a strange woman. She was too elegant for Gilbert, South Dakota, in her beige linen shorts and white knit shirt. She was also pale, with dark shadows below her big hazel eyes. Those eyes looked a little empty, like her soul was tucked far away inside her, too far to be seen. Until she'd laughed, she'd looked so sad he'd almost wanted to fold her into his arms and whisper that everything would be okay.

He didn't like thinking that about a woman who had just cost him a dream.

Blue knew himself to be a soft touch when it came to sad-eyed women, and he knew that if he didn't call his dog, Shoonk, and go now, he was going to get a lot more involved with this woman and her problems than was smart. Faced with a hurting soul, he rarely turned away, and the tendency had proved his downfall more than once. Lately, he'd been doing better about abandoning his own dreams and plans to salve someone else's pain, but right now he could feel concern for Shelley Mathews rising in him, competing with his anger and frustration over losing the house to her. It was a concern he didn't need.

"I don't have a plight," he finally said.

"Technically, we both do," she said softly. "You just lost the house you thought you'd rented, and I'm going to feel as guilty as a graffiti artist caught with the spray can in hand if I take it. There's only one house and two of us who need it. If we share it, then we can both lose our plights."

"We'd gain another one."

Shelley frowned. "What would that be?"

"Small-town gossip."

Chapter Two

Shelley regarded him with cool aplomb. "That doesn't bother me."

"Ever experienced it?"

Shelley thought of the news reports of her husband's death, the reporters shoving microphones and cameras in her face as she left the hospital, the sensational headlines, the interviews with her family and friends. She thought of how she'd gone through it all again at the trial a year later.

"Something similar." Her voice sounded flat, even to her own ears.

"People would talk if we shared the house."

Shelley could tell from the way he widened his stance that this was important to Blue.

"They'll say you just came out here to snag an Indian boyfriend. Folks'll talk."

She lifted a shoulder in gentle dismissal. Derision

would be easier to bear than pity. She'd survived pity; she could tolerate anything.

"Your students may be disrespectful," he added.

"I can handle my students."

He didn't give up. "This isn't the city. There's no anonymity here. If you drive into town to buy ketchup at nine o'clock on Saturday night, somebody notices and wonders why you need ketchup that late at night. If you've been here a week, you can bet a lot of people already know your car, who you are and which places you've tried to rent. If I live in this house with you, every person on the rez will have something to say about it."

"This would bother you more than it would me."

Blue shifted his weight, then stood straighter. "Looks like it would."

"Why?"

"I want joint custody of my kids. I don't want social services thinking I won't give them a good home, and I don't want my mom and my aunts worrying about my morals. I have a reputation in this community that I've worked hard for. I don't want it trashed for no good reason."

Shelley conceded his point with a nod. "Can't we make it clear that this is not a romantic relationship?"

"Out here, men and women don't live together unless they're involved."

"I'm sure some have."

"Not that I ever heard of."

"With this kind of housing shortage?"

He shrugged. "That's the way it is. People live with family."

"Isn't there something we could do to quell the gossip?"

"Oh, sure." He chuckled. "We could get married. After the initial buzz, things would settle right down."

Much to her consternation, Shelley had a sudden, graphic vision of sharing the intimacies of marriage with this man. It was the first blatantly sexual thought she'd had in so long, she blushed.

"I don't think that will be necessary," she said quickly.

Blue had the nerve to laugh at her. Pleasure lighted his face, and a smile lingered in his snapping dark eyes.

"Probably not," he teased. "Don't look so worried."

"I'm only worried about sorting out this housing situation. I showed up at the wrong time for you. If we shared the house, in a year, as you pointed out, I'll probably be gone. Then you would have the advantage of being established here. I doubt Mr. Heber would make you move. Could you stand a year of gossip to get the place all to yourself?"

Blue thought about that for a while. When Shelley saw resignation flicker through his expression, she knew he had made a decision.

"Do you drink or smoke? Use any drugs?"

They were perfunctory questions. He would stay. Her conscience eased.

"I have a glass of wine with dinner sometimes. That's all."

He nodded. "Good. I don't drink much, either. I have relatives who smoke. Some of them are elders. If they came over, I wouldn't ask them to go outside."

"That's fine." She'd noticed that a lot of people smoked here. Luckily, it didn't bother her too much.

"I'll have family who'll drop by. And my kids will come for Christmas and some other holidays."

"Of course. How old are they?"

Blue spoke with quiet pride. "Libby's thirteen and Travis is nine. They're good kids, but Libby's been having a hard time with her mom. She's growing up faster than Carlene wants her to."

"I like children. Anything else?"

"I like it real quiet most of the time," Blue warned. "I have tough courses this fall, and I'll need to study at home. No parties."

Shelley thought of the vast silences her life had held for the past four years. "Quiet is fine with me."

"I hate rap music," Blue added.

The blood drained from Shelley's face. Once again, for what seemed like the millionth time, she heard the harsh rhythms of the rap song that had blasted from a sidewalk boom box when she discovered her husband lying dead in the street.

"What's wrong?" Blue asked immediately.

She should tell him if they were going to be roommates—not yet, though.

"Um, no rap music," she stammered. "That's fine. It has bad associations for me, anyway."

Blue watched her for long seconds, and Shelley felt like he saw too much. She didn't want him to see her pain, to feel the emptiness inside her, and she certainly didn't want to talk about it right now. There would be time enough later.

Fortunately, Blue didn't pursue the questions that were in his eyes.

"Well, okay, I guess," he said with a sigh. "You're right—it's not a perfect solution, but we can try it."

"Good." She stuck out her hand to shake on it.

Blue accepted her hand, and again she felt his warmth and strength, along with a small buzz of awareness that made her stare at their joined hands. His wide palm engulfed hers, his thick fingers masculine against her own, his touch sure and easy.

Not letting go, Blue made one last stipulation. "We have to have open communication. If anything is bothering either one of us, we'll talk about it up front. Okay?"

"Yes," Shelley agreed. "I'd like that." A thought occurred to her. "I don't mean to pry, but it could affect how we work things out. Do you have a girlfriend?"

Blue shook his head. "Last one moved to Phoenix a year ago. I don't think I'll have time this fall for much of a social life. What about you?"

Shelley pulled her hand away from him. "What do you mean?"

"Do you date much?"

Shelley's hair swung with her emphatic denial. "No. I'm…" She was about to say she wasn't ready yet, but that Pandora's box could wait. "No."

"We'll sort out privacy requirements as we go, I guess."

She nodded, not quite meeting his eyes.

Blue laid one hand on the porch rail and looked at the house, a bittersweet longing on his face. "I hope this works out."

"I think it will be fine." It was an automatic thing to say. She didn't know him at all. She *hoped* it would be fine.

"Let's go pick out our rooms, then," he said, waving her ahead of him up the steps.

At eight-thirty that evening, Blue stood at the western edge of the yard, watching a pair of white-tailed deer pick their way across the alfalfa field toward the deep shadows of old windbreak of cedar, lilac and elm. Shoonk fidgeted at his side, then whined impatiently.

"Stay," Blue commanded. "Let those two be."

Shoonk sat with a huff, regarding Blue with mournful eyes. Then the screen door creaked, and man and dog turned to watch Shelley Mathews hang a wet rag to dry on the aluminum porch railing. She paused when she saw them, as if unsure whether or not to join them.

A pang of guilt assailed him. He hadn't been very nice to her today. Granted, he'd had cause to be out of sorts, but she wasn't responsible for Melvin Heber's behavior. He knew that. He also knew, taking in her graceful legs, noticing the way the last rays of the sun cast her in hon-eyed light, that one of the reasons he felt badly about having been less than a complete gentleman was that he was strongly attracted to her. Damn, if he didn't tingle all the way up his arm and right into his belly when he touched her. He wasn't surprised that he felt protective toward her, what with her sad eyes, grief-laden smiles and his own weakness for hurting souls, but those tingles had surprised him. They didn't have much at all to do with feeling sorry for the woman.

Not that he wasn't familiar with sexual chemistry. A lot of women found him attractive, and he'd liked a lot of women in return. Before his marriage and after his divorce, there'd never been any shortage of women willing to spend a little time with him. But this...this was different somehow. It was more than sexual, more than empathy, he thought, and he didn't know why that was when he didn't know her at all.

Blue felt like Shelley's voice penetrated the walls of each cell in his body. Her presence alone seemed to command his body's attention. All afternoon, as he worked to clean up the yard and the shed where he was going to keep his horses, Blue had sensed her every movement through the house. He'd think, *Oh, she's in the back bedroom now,* and look up to see her washing the windows in the back bedroom. He'd think, *She's in the living room,* and then he'd hear the vacuum she'd borrowed from Mr. Heber roar to life through the open living-room windows. It was almost spooky. Blue couldn't decide if he liked feeling so riveted by Shelley Mathews or if he wanted to run like hell.

He shouldn't want a woman he'd just met like this, especially not one that had cost him an independence he'd dreamed of for years, and especially not a woman who would be here a year and then gone. He most especially shouldn't be so attracted to this woman who had looked at him a few times today with something akin to lust in her pretty eyes. And damn if he didn't think she had no idea that was what she was feeling. The two or three times he thought he'd seen an appreciative flash in her eye, she'd immediately looked confused. Once she'd even blushed. Then she'd turned around and had been as cool as old smoke when he prodded her about what people might think if they shared the house.

Blue wondered where he and Shelley Mathews were going to end up when school was out next May.

Without consciously deciding to, he beckoned to her.

"There are some deer in the field." He spoke softly, his invitation carrying in the still evening air.

Shelley crossed the rough grass to stand at his side. She wasn't easy with him, holding her chin a little too high, her shoulders a little too straight.

"Where?"

He pointed toward the windbreak. "Along the north edge, almost in the trees. A buck and a doe."

It took Shelley a few seconds to find them. "Oh. I see."

They watched as the buck raised his antlered head to scent the air. Shelley was close enough that Blue could smell her. Underneath the tang of household cleaners, she smelled of flowers and summer heat. Like the buck, he breathed deeply.

"Do they live in those trees?"

Blue shook his head. "No. There's no open water here. They're just passing through." Like Shelley, he thought. Just passing through.

"I finished scrubbing the cupboards," she said, her eyes still on the deer. "Do you still want to go to Rapid City tomorrow?"

Blue set aside thoughts of sexual chemistry for practical concerns. He'd been collecting housewares and furnishings for almost two years. He had an old tan couch his last girlfriend, Nadine, hadn't wanted to haul to Arizona, a simple pine desk, a beat-up table and some folding chairs. He had four place settings of brown-rimmed stoneware from the Alco in Arrowhead, a box of mismatched glasses from the used-furniture store in town, some old silverware one of his aunts had purchased with Betty Crocker coupons thirty years ago and a stack of blankets and quilts he'd received at giveaways over the past few years.

That left a lot he didn't have. Shelley didn't have a thing except some books and clothes. After getting the utilities set up that afternoon, he'd suggested they go to Rapid City, where the stores had a better selection and lower prices than anything Gilbert had to offer.

"Yeah," he said, answering her question and admiring the curve of her jawline. "I think so. If we take the pickup, we can get a lot of stuff back without having to wait for a delivery.''

"I was thinking I might buy a washer and dryer.'' Shelley tentatively placed a hand on Shoonk's head. The dog closed his eyes and leaned into it. "The Laundromat in town didn't look very clean.''

"It isn't.'' Blue thought her touch was wasted on Shoonk.

"I need a bed and a desk,'' she continued. "Maybe a chest of drawers. I didn't realize it would be so hard to find decent used furniture out here.''

"We may have to have some stuff delivered.''

He liked the way that sounded—*we*. At the same time, it made him nervous.

Shelley seemed oblivious to his distraction, completely unaware of his response to her. "It sounds like it.''

The deer moved into the trees, out of sight, and Shelley turned her gaze to him.

"Shall we make a list of all the things that need doing and any supplies we'll need? You mentioned that you wanted to paint the living room and bedrooms, so we'll need paint, brushes and rollers. Then we can decide what household items we need.''

Then he saw it again, that little flash of awareness, the almost imperceptible widening of her pupils that told him she wasn't immune to him. And sure enough, right on its heels came a baffled lift of her brows and a tiny shake of her head.

Blue smiled. "That's a good idea.'' It was amazing how his brain could keep track of a conversation while his body was attending to all sorts of other information. "You know, I'm not happy Heber yanked this place on me this morning, but I think it might work out okay sharing the house.''

Shelley gave him a grateful smile. "I think so, too. I'm sorry about what happened. I know I sort of forced myself into your life..." She let the sentence hang unfinished.

Blue waited deliberately, holding her gaze. Then he touched her lightly just above the elbow. "I think I have room in my life for a new roommate."

For a moment, pleasure chased away the shadows in her eyes, and sweet tingles rippled up Blue's arm.

"Thank you." She stepped away from him, breaking the connection. "Let's get that list started, shall we?"

He followed her back into the house.

Two hours into the ride to Rapid City the next day, Shelley found herself in the middle of the Badlands. Stark formations of pale rock rose ahead of her as Blue drove into the tiny town of Interior. A drive-in advertised Indian tacos. A couple of RVs sat in front of the single gas station. A line of pickups had pulled up to the old hitching rail in front of the bar.

Shelley took it in, but didn't say much. Blue had done most of the talking on the drive, telling her about the communities they had passed, about this butte or that creek, but he was silent now.

Yesterday afternoon, she'd asked Steve Skillman, the high-school principal, about Blue and gotten a glowing report and a little info. She knew he'd had an ugly divorce, and that he was the best cross-country coach the high school had ever had. Shelley could tell that Skillman both liked and respected Blue. She didn't know much more about him than that. He didn't know any more about her, yet here they were, on a shopping trip to furnish the house they were sharing. It would be a good time to tell him a little more about herself, although she wasn't sure where to start.

Blue must have been thinking along similar lines.

"Since we're going to be roommates, maybe we should get to know each other a little better," he said.

His eyes were on the road, not her, and Shelley found it easier to answer that way. "That's a good idea."

"What do you want to know about me? I don't keep too many secrets. You can ask me pretty much anything, and I won't take offense."

Shelley smiled a little. He was so open. She had been that way once, but it seemed like a very long time ago.

"Where did you grow up?"

"On the Turtle Creek rez. My family lived in Lodge-pole. It's about ten miles north of Gilbert, where the old agency headquarters was. The tribal-government offices are there now."

He told her more about the history of the agency and the reservation and his family. Brad would have loved listening to Blue, she thought. He hadn't always remembered what people told him, but he had always wanted to hear all about everything. He would have had two dozen questions for Blue. Shelley had to think hard to come up with each one.

"Have you always lived there?"

Blue shook his head, eyes still on the winding road. "No. I left when I was eighteen to go to college in Denver. I had a scholarship, but I didn't make it through my first year. I had a lot of trouble with the classes. But mostly, I didn't fit in with all those kids whose fathers were dentists and accountants. Before the end of the spring semester, I dropped out and rode rodeo bulls for a few years."

"Professionally?"

Shelley was surprised. This morning he'd gone for an early bike ride, dressed in bike shorts and a chartreuse Lycra shirt, with a baseball cap turned backward on his head. He'd looked so contemporary, so hip. Even though she knew he had horses, she hadn't thought of him as a cowboy.

Blue laughed. "Yep. I'm a cowboy from way back. My dad worked on a ranch near Lodgepole when I was a kid, and I spent every minute I could out there. I learned to ride bulls and broncs well enough to keep me in gas money and beer for a while. My fourth year in, I tore up my knee and gave it up. I'd met Carlene by then, so I thought I was ready to settle down and start a family. We got married and moved to Casper. She had family there."

"What did you do for a living?" That was an easy question.

"Worked at Flair." He named a national chain of discount department stores. "I worked my way up to assistant manager. Had me a nice new Ford pickup, two great kids, a nice little house. It wasn't a bad life."

"What happened?"

Blue frowned, but he kept talking in the same easy tone. "Carlene and I had some problems. We were real young when we got married, had Libby right away. Like a lot of people, we got busy and didn't notice for a while that we were growing apart." Blue paused for a few seconds. "What happened, though, was that I got more involved than I should have with a woman who worked for me at the store. She'd had a tough time, lost her kids in a messy divorce with an abusive guy who wouldn't leave her alone. Carlene thought I was having an affair with her. I wasn't, but I was spending a lot of time with this other woman. Her name was Karen.'' He sighed. ''She needed someone. I was worried about her.''

Shelley didn't say a word. The highway wound through a river valley, the sheer, rocky walls of the Badlands neatly fencing the far side of the pastures where cows grazed. She stared at the road and the cattle, anywhere but at Blue.

''Carlene was working at a bank,'' Blue continued. ''She started sleeping with one of the vice presidents when she thought I was having an affair. Turned out she liked him a lot better than me. She kicked me out, then called my boss and told him I was screwing around with one of the employees. The store had a policy of no fraternization between employees, and my boss was worried about sexual-harassment charges since I was Karen's superior. He talked to me about it and I tried to explain, but he was a straight-arrow kind of guy. Once Carlene said I was sexually involved with Karen, I was guilty until proven innocent.

''Then Carlene told her friends, word got out and Karen felt so bad she left town. Karen did things like that on impulse, without thinking them through. She told me once all she ever did was cause trouble for people.'' He shook his head. ''I don't know what happened to her. Anyway, she ended up causing trouble for me because she wasn't around to tell people the truth. My boss was sorry about it, but he fired me anyway. Most folks thought it was over sexual harassment.''

''I'm sorry.'' Shelley knew the stigma accusations of sexual harassment carried, true or not. It was hard to fight, impossible to overcome professionally. ''Is that when you came back to the reservation?''

''Yeah. That was five years ago. I was broke. I'd lost my job, my family, everything. I had to get my clothes from the thrift store in Lodgepole and stay with my cousin. But I promised myself I would make a life I could be proud of again. I want to be a father my kids can be proud of.''

Shelley didn't respond. She thought about how hard it must have been for Blue to leave his children.

He didn't seem to need a response. ''The worst of it all was having the kids not really understand why I left. It's still hard. Once last year, Libby asked me if I'd really sexually harassed that woman. I hate the thought of them hearing lies about me. I hate not being there all the time to show them who I am, to answer their questions. To love them. Carlene thinks it's all water under the bridge, but I'm still living apart from my kids. I'm still trying to build another life that they don't have to be ashamed of.''

Shelley swallowed hard. Blue had been doing what she needed to do—building a new life. Face-to-face with ill fortune and human weakness, he hadn't given up. Suddenly, she wanted to know more about how he'd done that. ''Why did you come back to the reservation?''

''Indians always come back to the rez.'' His laughter was low and sweet. ''My mom and my aunts and my cousins were still here. My brothers are off in Denver or Minneapolis. One's an attorney, two work for the federal government. I couldn't afford to live in a city. So I came back, enrolled at the tribal college and decided to get myself a B.A. in business. I already knew quite a bit from working in the store, but with a degree, I'll have a lot more options. Besides—'' he flashed a smile at her ''—I like it out here. I don't want to leave again.''

''How did you...?'' Shelley wasn't quite sure what she wanted to ask. She tried again. ''How did you know what to do? How did you know to go back to school?''

''I didn't at first. I just came back, and I knew I didn't

want to sit around feeling sorry for myself, doing nothing. There aren't any jobs anywhere for a guy with no references and rumors of sexual harassment not very far behind him. If I didn't want to go nuts, I had to do something. So I made a plan, and I followed it.''

"A plan." That simple. Maybe he could help her with a plan for getting a life. She'd been working on instinct, choosing a place completely different from San Diego, but beyond the move and the new job, she didn't know what else to do. She needed a plan.

Blue thought for a minute, then spoke again. "Maybe it wasn't that clear cut. I came back because I knew people would accept me here, no matter what had happened. I decided I would be open about what happened, tell my side of the story, not make it some big secret. Then I didn't let myself hide from the past. I made myself keep moving forward. I joined a softball league. I signed up for classes. I helped my cousins work their horses and get their houses ready for winter. It wasn't until after I talked to some of my relatives and some of the people at the college that I really had a Plan, with a capital *P*.''

"Maybe that's what I need," Shelley mused. "A Plan with a capital *P*.''

"Why is that?" he asked.

Chapter Three

Their eyes met in a quick glance, then each one looked back at the highway. Blue waited, wondering if Shelley would answer.

"I need a new life," she finally said.

"You said that yesterday. Why?"

When she was silent, he reached across the seat between them and oh-so-lightly rubbed his index finger on her shoulder. It was a fleeting gesture.

Another darting glance revealed Shelley's grim expression. Uh-oh, Blue thought. That was not a healthy-looking face. Her gaze was fixed forward, but he didn't think she was aware of anything but her own thoughts.

"It's hard for me to talk about," she eventually answered. "I haven't told very many people. In San Diego, everyone already knew."

She took a deep breath, then spoke quickly, in the flat voice he was coming to recognize. "I pretty much had a normal life growing up. I'm an only child. My dad is an executive for an insurance company. My mom was a nurse, but she hasn't worked outside the home for a long time. I grew up in San Diego, and I went to UCLA. I became a teacher against everyone's advice, but I love it."

She took another slow breath. "I got married right after college. Brad, my husband, was going to be a doctor, and we moved back to San Diego because he got accepted to medical school there. I taught, he studied. We had a lot of friends."

Shelley sighed from the depths of her soul, and Blue knew what was coming. He didn't know the specifics, but instinctively, he knew her loss was greater than that of a divorce.

In the same flat voice, she went on. "My husband was killed in a drive-by shooting four years ago. He was picking me up at a homeless shelter where I volunteered every week. I was a little late that night, and Brad waited for me in front of the building, talking with some of the kids who hung out on the street there." A small pause. "Brad was killed by a fifteen-year-old gang member."

Blue wanted to slow the pickup, pull off the road and take her into his arms. Her matter-of-fact tone ripped at his guts. He knew, though, from the rigid set of her shoulders that she didn't want his comfort.

He gave what he thought she would accept. "I'm sorry, Shelley."

"Thank you." She watched a hawk glide lazily over the road. They passed it quickly. "I stopped living when my husband died. I moved back to my parents' house. I went back to my job after six months, but I didn't do anything else. I stopped seeing our friends." Another pause. "I got lost."

He was afraid she was still lost. Oh, God, it was Karen all over again. Only this time, he wanted this lost soul's body with the devil's own passion. Maybe he should be tougher with her than he'd been with Karen.

"Four years is a long time to be lost."

He saw her solemn nod out of the corner of his eye. "I know. That's what my parents and my therapist said, too. For the first two years, everyone treated me with kid gloves. Then they started getting impatient. People think there's some magic point at which you should naturally start feeling better. When you lose a spouse like that, they tell you it'll take a couple of years before you start to really move on. But it's taken me longer than that. Finally, my dad kicked me out." She laughed a little. "My mother was horrified when he told me I had to move out before the next school year started."

"How about you? Were you horrified?"

"No." Her voice sounded firmer, less woebegone, less lost. "Actually, I was grateful. He was right. I need to move forward. I loved Brad, but he's gone. The senselessness of his death still makes me angry, but I can't change what happened. So here I am." She spread her hands. "Starting a new life in South Dakota."

Blue frowned. "An Indian reservation can be a pretty tough place. Do you think it's the best place for this new life?"

"I don't know."

Blue doubted it.

"It worked for you," she said.

"I was born here, raised here. My family's here. I'm Lakota, and this is my home, but I don't kid myself. As much as I love it here, life on the rez can be hard."

"I'm not sure it can be any harder than losing Brad was."

"I hope you're right."

He didn't know why he was talking to her like this instead of offering reassurance. He was worried about her. Anyone who was still in this much grief four years after losing her husband didn't strike him as being up to facing the violence and hardship she might encounter on the rez.

"Blue, why is life harder on the reservation than other places?"

"You saw some of the racism yesterday."

Shelley nodded slowly.

"There's a lot of poverty," he continued. "It's hard to watch. You'll want to do something, but you won't have the resources to help everyone. Then there are the so-called social problems."

"Such as?"

She sounded cool, detached. That wouldn't last—not after she met her students and saw what some of them had to cope with.

"Alcoholism. Abusive family situations. The loss of Lakota culture and all the ways that affects people's lives."

"You make it sound bleak."

"It isn't always, but it can be. Do you think you'll be able to take it when it is?"

"I don't know."

Shelley didn't seem to know much, and that annoyed Blue.

"I thought you said you wanted a Plan with a capital *P.*"

"Mmm. I do."

"I think you should think about what you want to do. Think about whether you can handle a whole year out here. There are lots of easier places to make your new life, Shelley. You could make a good plan a lot of other places.''

''You're trying to get rid of me,'' she accused gently.

He shook his head. ''No. I like you. I think it may be interesting sharing the house with you.'' He deliberately avoided saying *living with you,* even though he thought it. ''I'm a sucker for a woman with a grieving past. I want you to feel better, be stronger, find that new life you want. But I don't want you to be surprised. I don't want you to leave in worse shape than you came.''

A quick glance showed him her sad smile. ''You don't have to worry about me.''

''Somebody has to.''

''No, they don't.'' She looked at him. ''But thank you. You have a kind heart.''

''You don't know the half of it, Shelley.''

Her smile warmed. She was oblivious to the fact that he was so attracted to her. She suspected no ulterior motive in him, saw nothing but a generous heart.

He gave her his best smile, the one that his grandma had forbidden him to use when she made fry bread and *wojapi,* the same smile that had gotten him married at age twenty-two and made him a daddy at twenty-three.

Blue was rewarded with a wide-eyed stare followed by that eyebrow quirk and a tiny frown. Shelley Mathews may not have had much of a life since her husband's death, but she was heading right back into the thick of things. The first step in her new plan might involve a little flirtation just for the fun of it.

That, Blue thought, was one thing he could provide. Whether he should or not was very much open to question, but since when had he ever let caution dictate to him when there was a pretty woman in need of solace?

* * *

The next morning, Shelley woke up early to the sound of meadowlarks and blackbirds singing in the fields outside. A soft breeze floated in from the open windows, cool and moist, the last evidence of last night's mild thunderstorm.

Stretching, she lazily reviewed yesterday's activities. She and Blue had shopped until Shelley had thought she would collapse. When they finally finished at the mall, Blue had driven them about ten miles west of Rapid City into the Black Hills to a restaurant he liked. They'd eaten gigantic hamburgers in the stone lodge, then come back to town to do some grocery shopping.

Shelley hadn't realized how tired she was until she found herself nodding off as they sped back through the Badlands. When they finally reached the house and carried in the last of the bags, the first rumblings of thunder reached their ears. Shelley had fallen asleep to the light patter of raindrops, for the first night in memory, too tired to think, too tired to mourn.

That had to be good, she told herself, sitting up. The next few days would also be busy as she cleaned the house and prepared for the new school year. As she reached for her robe, Shelley smiled and shuddered briefly in unexpected relief. This was what she needed— to be so busy she didn't have time to think about anything.

In the kitchen, she unpacked the new coffeemaker and prepared a pot of coffee, then sat down at Blue's red Formica table to review the growing pile of lists she was accumulating. Today she wanted to start with getting the walls and ceilings ready to paint. Blue had said he would help when it was time to paint, and Shelley was looking forward to working with him. He was a good man, honest, direct and patient. And his smile was really something, full of mischief and fun and so very sexy.

Sexy? Oh, dear. But he was. Well, she didn't have to do anything about that. She would just appreciate it. They were roommates. It would invite complications if she paid too much attention to him as a man, even if she were ready for a little romance—which she most certainly wasn't.

The back door swung open, interrupting her thoughts. Shoonk bounded in, Blue right behind him. As he came through the entry into the kitchen, Shelley looked up, startled.

He breathed deeply and smiled. "Is that coffee I smell?"

He wore shorts and a T-shirt, and his hair was damp from an early-morning bike ride. Shelley's gaze swept over him, ending up on his legs. Strong and brown, his calves and thighs were cut with supple muscle, beautifully proportioned, inescapably male.

"Ah…" Her eyes flew back up to his, and she knew from the way his eyes crinkled and his mouth twitched that he'd caught her admiration. "Coffee." The machine gurgled and steamed as the last of the water drained into the filter. "Perfect timing." She smiled quickly, then looked back at her list. The image of him stayed in her mind's eye.

"Didn't we buy mugs yesterday?" Blue moved away from her, toward the coffeemaker.

"Yes. They're in the plastic bag with the place mats and napkins, I think."

"Bingo." He raised two dark blue mugs. Shelley started to rise. "No, stay there," he told her. "I'll get you a cup. How do you like it?"

"Black."

He poured their coffee, then joined her at the table. Shelley thought she felt a little wave of heat as he approached. Maybe it wasn't heat exactly, but it was something that made her feel more alive than she had in years.

"More lists?" He sipped his coffee. "Mmm. Strong." He headed back to the refrigerator. "Sure you don't want any milk?"

"Is the coffee too strong?"

When he leaned into the refrigerator, Shelley couldn't help noticing how nicely the cotton shorts stretched across his backside.

"It's fine. Can I get you anything while I'm up? Yogurt, maybe? Orange juice?"

"No, thanks. I'm fine."

As he sat down, he swiped his hand through his hair, drawing her attention to the sinewy strength of his forearm. Shelley itched to touch him and quickly picked up her coffee to give her hands something to do.

Blue sipped appreciatively. "Tell you what. I'll take a shower, then I'll cook breakfast. Do you like pancakes?"

Shelley nodded. "That sounds good. I guess we should talk about whether or not we want to have meals together sometimes."

Blue set his cup on the table and caught her gaze. "I'd like to have meals with you." He paused, his gaze a little too intent. It implied more than meals, and Shelley felt uncertainty rise from her gut.

Shoonk sidled up to nudge Blue's hand for an ear scratch. Blue smiled and the moment passed.

"As our schedules allow," he continued in a more neutral tone. "We'll see how things shape up once school starts. I'll warn you. I'm a bacon-and-eggs man, but only on special occasions—like days when I know I'm going to spend a hot afternoon painting. Gotta watch the old cholesterol.''

"You look pretty healthy to me," Shelley commented as lightly as she could, absolutely forbidding herself to glance at his body.

His knee bumped hers under the table, and she scooted quickly away. "My old man died of a heart attack when he was barely sixty. I want to be around to see my grandkids someday." He gulped the last of his coffee and rose. In a moment, he had disappeared into his room.

Shelley let out a breath she hadn't realized she was holding. Blue Larson was a very easy man to like, but it wouldn't do to be quite so fascinated with him. She needed to keep things on a friendly but platonic level with him. If they got involved and it didn't work out, where would she live? The house was the important thing, having a stable base, a safe haven. Determined to ignore anything that might put that at risk, she finished her list, then went to change into comfortable clothes for the day's work.

At noon, Blue and Shelley shared sandwiches and cold drinks and chatted about their progress with the house and the outbuildings. Blue had the corral pump working and the fence repaired. He kept the conversation light and didn't give her any more of those looks like he had over coffee. He knew she was both aware of him and uncomfortable with that awareness.

But, he reminded himself, he should go slow with Shelley. Become friends first. See if there was more than sexual interest.

Watching her finish her drink and lick her lips, he suppressed a smile. There was more. He knew it in his belly and in his heart. How much more, he wasn't sure, but he knew her sad smiles had hooked his interest on a number of levels. He wanted to lighten her sorrow, chase away the distance built through years of grief and pain. More than anything, he wanted to be a damn hero, to save her from loneliness, to help her find life again.

Half disgusted with himself for confusing friendship with something more intimate, Blue scooted back from the table and rose.

Shelley looked up immediately. "Is something wrong?"

Nothing a good shrink couldn't fix in ten years or so. "No. Just ready to get started painting." He carried their plates to the sink.

"Where do we start? Walls or ceilings?"

"Ceilings. Let me take down the ceiling fans and light fixtures."

"I'll get the drop cloths. Everything's taped already."

Blue did smile then. Shelley was thorough in her preparations. The walls were clean, the window and door frames, the baseboards, and any other woodwork taped, and everything put away. The wooden ladder they'd bought the day before was in the living room. The cans of paint, brushes, rollers, and paint trays were lined up against the living room wall.

"I'll clean the dishes while you get the fixtures down," she offered.

She stood beside him at the sink and reached for the plates. Without thinking about it, he angled himself closer to her, allowing his forearm to brush hers. She froze. When she started to move away, he put the plates in her hands, purposely brushing his fingers against hers.

"I'll get the ladder," he said, forcing himself to move away.

Shelley gave a quick nod and turned on the faucet.

Throughout the afternoon, Blue looked for little ways to touch her. He told himself not to do it, but when she got close to him, he couldn't help it. His brain told him to keep his distance, but his body paid no attention.

When they got to the living room, Shelley looked skeptically at the acoustic ceiling. "Maybe I should start on the walls in my bedroom."

"No, no." Blue screwed his roller onto an extension pole and motioned for her to do the same. "It's not hard."

He dipped his roller into the paint tray to demonstrate. "Nice and easy. Enough, but not too much." He raised the roller above his head with no drips. "Sometimes it takes a bit of dabbing."

When he glanced at Shelley, she was watching him instead of the paint going onto the ceiling. He let her look for a moment before he lowered the roller.

"Okay. Think you can handle it?"

She knit her eyebrows in a worried look.

Without thinking, Blue took her roller from her and put it down. "Come here." He hooked her arm and pulled her in front of him, then fitted his roller into her hands and stepped closer. Covering her hands with his, he guided the roller back into the paint tray. He wasn't quite pressing into her, but he could feel every inch of her, from the soft curve of her backside to the whisper of her bare calf brushing his own. She was warm and soft, and she fit perfectly in his arms.

"Just like this." Somehow his head knew to keep talking about painting. "Enough, but not too much."

He raised their arms and applied the paint-filled roller to the ceiling. Her arms were warm next to his, and she smelled of flowery shampoo and warm woman, a scent that penetrated right through the acrid smell of the paint. "This is perfect."

Shelley wriggled, trying to put some distance between them. Instead, her rear end collided with the front of his jeans. Blue had been aroused before. Now he ached.

"Okay. Think you have the feel for it?" He sounded cooler than he felt.

Shelley was flustered, barely able to speak. "Mm-hmm. Yes, I think so."

Blue took the roller from her. Once more, without thinking, without realizing what he meant to do until it was done, he turned her to face him.

Her eyes were wide with that startled-doe look, her eyebrows drawn together in puzzlement. "Blue..."

When her lips puckered to say his name, he dipped his head to kiss her. It was a quick kiss, no more than a press, a shy taste of her lower lip, a hand on her shoulder. He forced himself to stop, to stand back.

Shelley never closed her eyes. When her tongue flicked out to lick the lip he had just kissed, the blood pounded in his head. He started to back up, but she stayed him with a hand on his chest.

"I don't think we should do this." Her eyes dropped to study her hand on his chest. When she looked back up, the confusion was gone. She was cool again, composed. He wasn't. His heart thudded under her touch.

"No, we shouldn't. I'm sorry if I offended you."

Her hand stayed still on his heart. "You didn't offend me."

"It's because of the house."

She nodded, taking the easy answer he offered. "We both need it. If things got complicated..."

"I know." And he did. He also knew things were going to get complicated. He covered her hand with his and gave it a squeeze. "I'll behave. You're a beautiful woman, though. You make it tough."

She smiled and pulled her hand free. "Thank you. You're a handsome man, but this just isn't wise. I think I'll go ahead and work on the closet in my bedroom, after all."

Blue let her go, wishing she wouldn't, but knowing she should. He had to get control of himself. He was acting like a high-school kid, and he knew better. This wasn't what Shelley wanted from him right now. She was, however, far from indifferent to him. She'd liked the small kiss, and she'd liked touching him. She thought he was handsome.

It was a start, he thought, dipping the roller back into the paint. It was a start.

Chapter Four

The next several days passed without any more touches or sweet kisses from Blue. Shelley avoided him the first day, spending most of her time at the high school. The second day she stayed at the house to wait for the delivery of the washer, dryer and beds, organizing the cupboards while she waited. Blue spent the morning at the tribal college and worked outside in the afternoon. He spent both evenings with friends and relatives in Lodgepole.

By the third day, Saturday, Shelley had begun to feel both safe and, if she was honest with herself, a bit lonely. It had been so nice talking and working with Blue, enjoying his companionship—and, since she was being truthful, his flirting.

On Sunday morning, Shelley caught Blue on his way out with Shoonk for a bike ride.

"I thought I'd make breakfast this morning, since it's the last day before school starts again. Interested?"

Blue stopped with his hand on the door. Shoonk whined, anxious to go. "Sure. What's on the menu?"

"How does French toast sound?"

He grinned. "Best offer I've had all week. I'll be back in an hour or so."

By the time he returned, sweat trickling out of his hair, his clothes plastered to his body, Shelley had the table set with the new dishes and silverware and a small vase filled with hollyhocks from the yard. The grapefruit halves sat in pretty glass bowls, the coffee was brewing and two frying pans—one filled with bacon and the other with French toast—sizzled on the stove.

Blue breathed deeply. "I think I found heaven," he said. "Wow. And I thought I was a good cook. This spread looks great. Do I have time for a shower?"

Shelley nodded. "Everything will be ready in ten minutes."

He gave her that smile, the really sexy one, and she was glad to have the stove to lean on. Just ignore it, she told herself. They were roommates, nothing more.

When Blue came back, however, dressed in worn jeans that did little to hide the muscular strength of his legs, and a snug T-shirt, Shelley found she wasn't able to completely ignore the pleasure she took in looking at him. He smelled good, too, damp and fresh from the shower, the herbal scent of soap discernible when he leaned close to her to snag a piece of bacon from the plate where it was draining.

"Sorry," he mumbled around a full mouth. "I can't help myself. I could eat a pound of this if I didn't know better."

Shelley had figured that out.

He took the coffeepot and filled both their mugs while she transferred the bacon and French toast to a platter, which she set on the table next to a bowl of blueberries and a small pitcher of maple syrup.

When they were both seated, Blue clinked his mug to hers. *"Bon appétit."*

Shelley busied herself filling her plate. "Are you ready for school to start?"

He nodded, his mouth too full to answer immediately. "This French toast is great," he finally said. "What's in it? Some kind of citrus?"

"Orange peel."

"It's fantastic. I'll have to tell Libby about this. French toast is one of her specialties. She'd like this." He took another bite. "And, yeah, I'm ready to get back to school. Three years down, one to go. I got all my textbooks Friday and set up my hours in the computer lab."

She'd noticed the computer on the desk in his room. "What do you do in the lab?"

"I maintain the college's web site and help teach people how to set up their own. One of the English instructors always has her class create a web site. I help with that sort of thing, too."

"I'm completely inexperienced on the web."

"You better get with it, teach. Your students will be running rings around you."

Shelley chuckled. "As far as technology goes, they always have. I noticed that the high school doesn't have the kind of library I'm used to working with. It might be time for me to investigate how to use the Internet to teach tenth-grade history."

Blue took another piece of French toast and two more pieces of bacon. "You should. If you need any help, I'd be glad to work on it with you. I'm at the high school most afternoons during the fall, anyway.''

"You are?'' Why did that both interest and alarm her? She already saw him every day, and in much more intimate circumstances. Like this. Sharing a Sunday-morning breakfast.

"I coach the cross-country teams."

"That's right. I'd forgotten."

"Do you have your class lists yet?''

"I picked them up Friday."

"If you let me take a look, I can tell you if you've got any of my athletes."

Shelley rose to get her class rosters and brought them to the table. Blue took them to look at while he continued eating.

"Jeremy Crow Chasing was the top freshman on the team last year. He's talented. A wonderful student, too, makes the honor roll every time. His family's from down at Red Creek, really traditional folks. Both of his folks work at the college. Really good people.'' He went through the rosters, pointing out a name here, one there, chatting about the students and their families, until he got to one name. He put down his fork and tapped the name with his index finger.

"Bethany Garreaux." He said the name quietly. "This girl is the most talented runner I've ever coached. She has a gift. With the right training and support, she could go all the way to the top."

"But?" Shelley prompted when he stopped.

Blue shook his head once. "Lots of problems at home. She doesn't get the support she needs. Her grades are bad, even though she's as sharp as a whip."

"Have you talked to her parents?''

"Yeah. Me and everyone from the principal on up to

the superintendent. Bethany lives with her mom. I don't know what happened to her dad. He left while I was away, I guess. Anyway, talking hasn't helped. Her mom drinks.'' He looked as if he was going to say more, then didn't.

Shelley had had several students with alcoholic parents over the years. ''I'll keep an eye on her.''

''She'll be one of the hard ones, Shelley.'' His voice was still soft. ''Bethany could be one of the ones to break your heart. She's bright and talented, but she's only fifteen and her life is already a mess. Take it from someone with more of a messiah complex than is healthy. She'll make you want to do something to help, and there probably isn't much you can do. Especially if she doesn't want help.''

He looked so sad, Shelley wanted to touch him, to offer comfort. Instead, she sipped her coffee. ''Maybe this will be a better year for Bethany.''

''I sure hope so.'' He didn't sound convinced at all.

The phone rang, interrupting them, and Shelley reached for it automatically.

''Hello?''

There was a short hesitation, then came a young girl's voice, tight with tears. ''Is my dad there? I mean, Mr. Larson?''

''He's right here.'' Shelley handed the phone to Blue. ''It's your daughter, I think.''

''Libby? You're up early for a Sunday morning. What's going on, punkin?''

Libby was clearly upset. Shelley took her coffee cup and went into the living room to give Blue some privacy. She'd learned that Sunday newspapers came in the mail on Monday, one of the inconveniences of rural South Dakota living, so she busied herself instead with looking through the magazine put out by the state's electrical co-ops.

Blue was silent for a long time, listening, making comforting noises, but he didn't leave the kitchen table. Shelley wasn't sure if she should go outside so she couldn't hear at all, but then she decided he would move if he wanted more privacy. It was a cordless phone.

When Blue began to speak, she could hear the strain in his voice. It appeared Libby had had some disagreement with her mother.

"I know I said I'd have a place for you guys soon, but I still only have visitation rights, Libby. Your mom isn't going to let you come out here yet. Besides, things didn't go quite as planned with the house. It may be a while before you kids can live with me."

There was another long pause before Blue asked to speak with his ex-wife. Shelley decided now would be a good time to take a little walk, after all.

Shoonk fell in step beside her when she started on the road that wound along the windbreak toward the fields beyond. She knew that if Blue had been living in the house himself, he would been able to have his kids live with him, at least part of the time. With her living in the house, she could understand why he wouldn't be comfortable bringing them here, even when he won joint custody. It really wasn't fair at all. Mr. Heber should have kept his word and let Blue have the house. Of course, she would be camping in the school yard if he had, but it hadn't been right.

Behind the windbreak, Shelley found a large field devoted to storing huge rolls of hay. They looked like giant pieces of shredded wheat stacked in long rows, two bales high. On the far side of the field, red and black cows with white faces grazed in a wide pasture. As she approached the barbed-wire fence that separated field from pasture, she could hear the flies buzzing around the cattle and smell the tang of manure. Fifty yards away, she spied a small prairie dog town Blue had told her about. The little animals scampered and yipped, then raced for their burrows when Shoonk slipped under the fence to chase them.

Shelley watched the cattle for a while, then explored the windbreak. There were several types of trees, most of them old and gnarled, but there were plenty of volunteer seedlings springing up, as well. She spent almost an hour poking around and picking wildflowers, including some of the pretty alfalfa flowers. When she couldn't hold any more in her hands, she went back to the house.

Coming through the arched gate into the yard, Shelley looked up when the screen door opened with a loud bang, bouncing hard against the metal porch railing. Blue shot out the door, his face contorted in a grimace, his hands raking back through his hair.

Shoonk barked and raced forward. Blue looked and saw them, lowering his arms, though his hands curled into fists.

In the moment before he dropped his gaze to the dog, there was no mistaking the pain and frustration in his eyes. He bent on one knee the rub Shoonk's ears, speaking quietly.

"It's all right, boy. Nothing's wrong."

The dog barked again, leaned into Blue, then leaped off the porch to chase a moth.

Blue rose, and Shelley climbed the steps to stand beside him. She nodded her head toward the dog. "He may believe nothing's wrong, but I don't. Are you okay?"

"I will be."

She paused. More than anything, she wanted to reach out to him, much as she had at breakfast, to lay a comforting hand on his arm, his back. Almost of its own volition, her hand acted on those feelings, finding his shoulder.

"I'm sorry that you don't feel you can bring your children here."

Their eyes met. "Don't be sorry for that."

She tried a tentative stroke over his shoulder blade. He didn't move. Emboldened, she did it again. "Well, I am. I heard part of your conversation. Do you want to talk about it?"

Blue leaned back against one of the poles that supported the gable over the porch, moving slowly so that he didn't dislodge her hand on his shoulder. Then he lightly grasped the hand holding the wildflowers and tugged her closer.

"Libby snuck out last night and didn't get back until dawn. Carlene isn't sure who she was with, but she thinks there were some older boys involved. She's worried, and so am I. Libby's just starting eighth grade. She's a little girl still."

"She probably doesn't think so."

He shook his head. "She sure doesn't. She's so mad at Carlene she wants to move out. I know why she's mad. It isn't just last night. Carlene isn't consistent. She lets the kids get away with murder one day, then nails them for little stuff the next. She and Libby fight about everything now. Paul, Carlene's husband, has started stepping in, trying to establish more order, and now Libby's furious with him, too. Paul laid down the law this morning, told her he was going to put bars on her window if he has to to keep her in. Put her on restriction until Christmas vacation." Blue gave a halfhearted chuckle. "Think I might be able to like that guy, after all. But Libby's really struggling. She thinks she can come live with me and everything will be perfect.''

"Do you think it would be better for her to be with you?''

"Yeah. I do.'' He rubbed his finger along her wrist. "It won't be easier for her, at least not at first. I'm a lot stricter than Carlene is, and it would be an adjustment for her. In the long run, though, I think she and Travis would both be happier with me. I just don't know how to make that happen.''

Shelley realized she was tracing circular patterns on Blue's shoulder with her fingertips, and that she didn't want to stop.

"Maybe by next summer,'' she said, her voice low. Next summer. When she would be gone.

Blue raised his hand to tip her chin up. His eyes were dark and serious. "As much as I want to have my kids living with me, I don't want you to leave.''

Her fingers stopped moving when his gaze dropped to her mouth.

"I want to kiss you,'' he whispered.

Chapter Five

Blue moved closer, sliding one hand along Shelley's side, under her raised arm, tipping her chin a little higher with the other.

She closed her eyes and swayed into him, resting the hand that held the flowers against his waist. Gently, his mouth touched hers. His lips were as soft as a morning breeze and warmer than the August sun. His touch was light, fleeting, a brush, a retreat, another sweep against her mouth.

Slowly, by barely perceptible degrees, he increased the pressure and movement of the kiss. The hand under her chin slid to her nape, experimentally lifting her hair, caressing sensitive skin. His other hand splayed in the middle of her back, firm, urging her to him. When her legs met his, it sent a wave of desire through her, and she made a small wanting sound.

Blue pulled back. "Okay?"

She nodded.

"Again?"

She tilted her head, offering him her lips.

This time his kiss was surer, and she felt the tension build in his back and shoulders as his arms shifted around her. He licked at her lower lip, as he had the day they painted the ceiling, but this time he didn't pull away. After long moments exploring the texture and taste of her, he closed his teeth over her lower lip and ran the tip of his tongue over the inside of it.

Shelley's mouth opened more fully with a quick gasp, and he was there, not pushing, not demanding, but right there, his tongue meeting hers in quick, darting forays. Just as she began to feel invaded, he retreated. Just as she missed the taste of him—coffee, blueberries, a hint of orange and his own savory something—he came back.

Shelley's senses were filled with him, from his kiss to the scent of his body. The solid weight of his limbs around her and under her hands made her nerve endings dance, striving, as it were, to collect each sensation, each scrap of feeling his touch generated. She moved closer to him, wrapping one arm around his middle, the other playing more widely over his back. His waist was narrow, firm. His kiss stole her breath. How could anyone be so gentle and so insistent at the same time?

"Excuse me..."

An unfamiliar voice vaguely penetrated the sensual haze.

Someone cleared her throat loudly.

Blue's mouth eased away from Shelley's, slowly, reluctantly. Shelley feathered one hand up his back and caught his hair, thinking to pull him back to her. Then she registered the woman standing at the bottom of the steps.

Both of them looked at her, unable to move. Shelley's body was on fire. If Blue let go, she would probably sink to her knees. When she realized her breasts were resting on his chest and that their hips were tightly pressed together, she tried to straighten. The movement made clear his arousal. He held her in place.

"Marilyn?" He blinked at the woman, then looked down at Shelley before his eyes cleared. "Damn. I forgot you were coming."

"So I can see." The woman's tone was dry.

She was fiftyish, tall, slender and dressed to the nines in a pale peach suit, stockings and heels. Her dark hair was arranged in short, helmet-styled curls, and she wore her long-suffering patience with the hormone-charged pair on the porch with a combination of tolerance and well-bred disdain. She reminded Shelley of the organist at the church she had gone to as a child, kind, wise to human frailty, but definitely on the starchy side.

Blue finally eased his grip, and Shelley stepped away from him. He sent her a worried look, then took her hand to lead her down the steps.

"Shelley, this is Marilyn Tall Feather. She works for the department of social services. She's been helping me with the paperwork I need to get joint custody of my kids." He swallowed hard. "Marilyn, this is Shelley Mathews. My, um…" He shot the woman an uncomfortable look.

Shelley figured he'd realized *roommate* didn't sound too convincing under the circumstances.

"We rent the house together," he finally said.

Marilyn Tall Feather arched one neatly plucked brow at him before extending her hand to Shelley. Shelley accepted it self-consciously.

"You're the new history teacher," Marilyn announced, looking her up and down the way a boot-camp drill sergeant might inspect a new recruit. "My nephew, Adam Two Charge, will be in your third-period class this fall."

Shelley didn't know quite how to respond. "I'll look forward to meeting him."

"Just let me know if you ever have any trouble with him."

Shelley pitied Adam if he didn't yet know enough to stay out of trouble with a relation like this in close proximity.

"I can see we have more to talk about than I realized, Blue," Marilyn said, fixing him with a stern look.

"Yeah. I guess we do. Why don't we go inside?" He ushered the woman up the steps and into the house.

"I imagine you had a hard time finding a place to live," Marilyn said to Shelley as they settled themselves in the living room. The room now boasted a used sofa and armchair, a coffee table made out of wooden shipping boxes and lace curtains that let the light in. A few posters by Native American artists hung on the walls. It was a simple, pleasant room. Shelley set her flowers on the packing crates.

"Yes, I did." Shelley wasn't sure how much to say.

"Would you like some coffee, Marilyn?" Blue offered.

"No, thank you. I can't stay long. Sit down, Blue."

He perched on the edge of the armchair.

Marilyn looked at Shelley. "I imagine Melvin Heber took one look at you and reneged on his agreement to let Blue rent this place."

"Yes, I'm afraid he did."

"That man dearly loves single women tenants. Especially teachers and nurses."

"That's what he said." Shelley picked at a loose thread on the sofa, then caught herself and dropped her hands into her lap.

"So the reasonable thing to do was to share the house, of course. I'm sure people do that sort of thing all the time in California." Marilyn seemed to know a lot about her.

"It seemed like the best solution," Shelley agreed.

Lifting her chin in Blue's direction, Marilyn looked aggrieved. "You know better."

"I tried to tell her." He looked at the floor.

"He did," Shelley said. "But I didn't think there was any good reason two adults couldn't be roommates. I still don't."

"Theoretically, you're right. But you are both healthy, attractive young people and you are obviously interested in each other. Now you find yourselves something more than roommates," Marilyn concluded.

"Not exactly..." Shelley began.

"No, that's not quite..." Blue said at the same time.

Marilyn merely looked from one to the other with her eyebrow raised artfully.

"Shelley," she began, "I believe Blue is a good candidate to gain joint custody of his children, so much so that I made a special trip to stop by to see his new home on my way back from church this morning. I know he's a fine young man. From what I've heard from Steve Skillman, you're an excellent teacher and an upstanding person, as well. While I know you won't want to hear this, I have to tell you both that the two of you living here together will not help Blue's petition. Especially not in light of what I saw when I arrived."

Shelley recognized Marilyn's tone. It was one she herself had used on more occasions than she cared to count when one or another of her students had, through simple high spirits or excess energy, landed in unanticipated trouble.

"Perhaps I should leave you two alone to talk." Shelley looked at Blue, then Marilyn.

"No." Marilyn placed a hand on hers. "I think you should hear this, too. Blue already knows that I'm a very old-fashioned sort of person. For instance, I don't believe in unmarried people living together in sin. I understand that isn't what you intended to do, but anytime a couple doesn't hear a car drive up a gravel road or a car door slam fifty feet away, I would have to say that's where they are headed." She looked at each of them, as if expecting an argument.

When she didn't get one, she went on. "If one of the unmarried people involved in the relationship is a parent, bringing his children into the home with a live-in girl-friend presents a number of potential complications. Conflicts are difficult enough to negotiate with legal steppar-ents. Through the years, I have observed that it is generally harder for children of divorced parents to deal well with their parents' live-in boyfriends and girlfriends than with stepparents. In Blue's case, Libby is already having a hard time with her mother and stepfather. She needs a great deal of consistency and stability. She needs commitment from the adults in her life." Marilyn looked at Shelley. "Are you ready to give that to her? Are you ready to give it to each other?"

Blue interrupted. "Marilyn, this is premature. We just—"

"Of course it is. But how would it affect Libby to bring her here now? The situation is far too ambiguous."

Shelley's stomach began to churn. "It wouldn't be good for her."

Marilyn's expression softened. "Even if you were married, you would have to think carefully about what Shelley's role would be with your children. You would have to work out ways to handle authority and conflict. There would be a lot of work for all of you."

"I should leave," Shelley said quietly.

Marilyn touched her hand. "Either that or you should go ahead and get married. Get started on building a stable relationship together. Then by the time Blue can legally have his children live with him, the two of you will be able to provide the kind of home they need. It wouldn't hurt Blue's chances at all to be remarried. In fact, it might hasten matters along."

Shelley didn't know whether to laugh or cry. The whole conversation was absurd. She'd known this man for a week. They'd flirted a little bit. That was it. One kiss on the porch, and a social worker had them married.

Marilyn seemed to have finished her lecture. "Blue, why don't you give me a quick tour of the house? Then I can get part of my report written. You can let me know what you two decide next week."

Blue rose to escort Marilyn through the house. Shelley picked up the wildflowers and went in search of something to put them in.

Just like that, she thought, filling a glass with water. Lose your home, or marry someone you've known only a week. She heard Marilyn making noises of approval in the bedroom Blue would have made Libby's. For him, the choice was far worse. Lose your children, or marry a woman with whom you've shared two little kisses and a week's worth of chores.

Blue and Marilyn came back through the kitchen. His mouth was drawn, his posture rigid.

"Marilyn, if I moved right out, how long would it take

for Blue's custody petition to be approved and all the legal hurdles crossed?''

"Several months yet, but probably less than a year in this case, since all of the parties are cooperating. Even with Carlene's cooperation, though, these things take a certain amount of time."

"Thank you." Shelley set the flowers on the windowsill. "I appreciate your being frank with me."

"I'm sure you'll make a good decision."

There was an awkward pause. Blue caught Shelley's glance, his face unreadable.

"Are you going to show me where you'll be keeping the horses?" Marilyn asked gently. "It was nice to meet you, Shelley. Until next time."

She nodded, attempting to return Marilyn's smile. Inside, she wasn't smiling at all.

Blue hadn't said much after Marilyn left, just grabbed his keys and told her he'd be back late. She had no idea where he'd gone. While she was worried about him, she was also glad of the time alone to think.

Her first thought was to pack her clothes and go back to the Jack Rabbit Motel, but when she'd called to see if they had a room, there were no vacancies. That stopped her. Surely she could stay at the house until she found someplace else. What difference would a few more days or even weeks make? Instead of packing, she began cleaning up the breakfast dishes. Looking around the room, she felt like crying. The little house had started to feel like home.

Blue had started to feel like home, too. He made her feel alive for the first time in years. After the time she'd spent floating through life numb, he touched her, made her want to come out of the fog. As she thought about it, she was grateful. She also wanted more. Standing in the middle of the kitchen, staring at her brand-new washer and dryer without seeing them, Shelley realized that she didn't want to leave, and it wasn't because of all the work she'd put into the house during the past week.

She wanted to stay because of Blue.

Leaving the dishes soaking in the sink, she wandered into the living room and curled up in the chair he'd occupied during Marilyn's visit. She was attracted to him, but not in love. Love was something that needed time to grow.

How much time? she wondered. She wasn't at all sure she ever wanted to love again.

No, she didn't want to love Blue or anyone else. During the past week, though, she thought she and Blue had become friends, and she knew she needed friends. If they were developing a friendship, she also knew it was due mostly to his efforts, to his gentle questions, his openness, his willingness to show himself to her and his easy acceptance of her grief. Instead of backing off when she didn't respond quickly or easily, he stayed and waited. He listened. He made room for her in his life. In turn, she was learning to make room for him.

It had been a long time since Shelley had tried to let a man into her life, even as a friend. This week she'd been less lonely, even when she hadn't seen much of Blue, than she had since Brad's death. Blue Larson was good for her. He made her feel good, and he was a good man.

Would it be so bad to be married to a good man again? Even if she wasn't in love with him?

Shelley sat in the chair, her legs tucked under her, a small pillow hugged to her chest, and thought about that.

Maybe Marilyn Tall Feather hadn't been being quite as ridiculous as Shelley had initially thought with all that talk about marriage.

It was evening before Blue returned to the house. After a day spent pretending to fish at a WPA dam tucked in the river breaks above Turtle Creek, he was no closer to knowing what to do. He was almost surprised to see Shelley's gray car parked by the gate. He'd thought she might be packed and gone by the time he got back. With no small amount of frustration, he also noticed that he was relieved she hadn't left.

Two things were clear to him. He couldn't do anything that might jeopardize his custody bid for Libby and Travis, and he wanted to live in this house with Shelley right now. He wanted to hold her again, kiss her until both of them were spinning with lust and then take her to bed. He wanted to make her laugh, chase away the sadness in her eyes.

Why now? Why her?

Everything was wrong.

Slamming the truck door to let her know he was back, Blue wondered if Heber would let him have the house if Shelley left. Not likely. As far as Heber was concerned, it would be Blue who should leave.

Shoonk bounded toward him, anxious for attention and unhappy at having been left behind all day. Blue scratched the dog's ears and belly, even threw Shoonk's tennis ball a few times, stalling. Finally, he gave him a last pat.

"Time for me to go in, boy."

The dog barked.

"Sorry." Blue pushed open the gate.

Inside, the lights were off, the house dark in the twilight shadows. Blue heard Shelley's voice, soft, relaxed. It took him a second to realize she was talking to someone on the phone.

"I need to go now, Mom. I'll talk to you next week." A pause. "I love you, too. Bye."

Shelley was on the couch in the living room, still holding the phone when he came through the entryway door.

"You're back." She put the phone on the packing-crate table.

He walked into the room, no more sure what to say than he had been when he'd left that morning.

Shelley looked out the window where the dying light hadn't quite given way to night. As she so often did, she looked distracted, unfocused. A small, sad smile played across her face.

"I guess we need to talk," he said, taking another step forward.

When she looked at him, her smile had disappeared. "Yes." She scooted over on the couch, making room for him.

Blue lowered himself carefully into the farthest corner from her and hunched forward, dangling his linked hands between his knees. "I don't know what to do, Shelley."

She didn't speak immediately, turning instead in her seat to face him, tucking her legs under her. He felt her watching him. "I almost left. I would have if the Jack Rabbit Motel had had any vacancies."

"I figured that." He stared at his hands. Not at her. That wouldn't help.

"I thought about what to do all day."

He nodded.

"It's a difficult situation, but the most important thing is your custody petition."

It was, but it wasn't so simple for him, and he didn't

know how to tell her that. "If anyone leaves, it will be me," he said instead. "The lease is yours. Heber rented to you."

"But I may be gone in a year. It would be a shame for you to lose the house."

"I'll find someplace else."

Shelley nodded, and seemed about to say something that wasn't coming easily.

He waited.

"I don't want you to leave." Her voice was barely louder than a whisper.

Blue straightened and turned his head to look at her. "I don't want you to leave, either."

Lips pursed, she nodded once, slowly. Once again he waited for her to continue.

"I haven't been so lonely this week." Another pause. "I feel like we're becoming...friends."

The statement made his heart ache. "Good friends, I think. I like you, Shelley."

A hint of a smile reappeared on her lips. "I like you, too."

He thought about the kiss that morning for the zillionth time that day. "More than friends, maybe?"

Another hesitation. "Maybe." Each word came out slowly. "That's what I want to talk about."

This time Shelley reached for his hand. He took hers in both of his and angled to face her more fully. Between them, their joined hands met on the empty cushion.

"I thought about this a long time, Blue. I thought about all the things Marilyn said. At first I thought she was crazy, but the more I thought, the more what she said made a certain amount of sense." Under his thumb, Blue felt her pulse accelerate. "About marriage."

The word dropped between them like a bird stricken in midflight.

Shelley didn't seem able to continue.

Finally, he could bear the suspense no longer. "What about marriage, Shelley?"

Eyes wide, her cool fingers curled into his palm. "I think we should seriously consider getting married."

Chapter Six

All day Blue had resisted thinking about marriage as a realistic option for them. He'd never have asked it of her. And yet, now that she had brought it up...well, it would certainly solve a few thorny problems. But it was crazy.

"You think it's a bad idea," she said when he didn't respond.

"I don't know what I think." He searched her face. "Why would you want to marry me, Shelley?"

"It's the most logical thing to do, given the circumstances."

True as that may be, it wasn't quite what he wanted to hear.

"I guess what I'm talking about is a marriage of convenience. A mutually beneficial arrangement."

He didn't like either phrase. "That seems pretty cold-blooded."

"No, I don't think so," she said earnestly. "Logical, yes."

That's what she'd said when she suggested they share the house. It was the "logical solution."

"But it isn't unemotional. I couldn't even think about doing it if it were. I like you. I respect you. Those are feelings. And there's—" She broke off.

"There's passion between us."

She lifted her chin in a jerky nod. "There's something, yes."

"But it isn't love."

She didn't contradict him.

"Shelley, it's too soon for us to know what we want to do. I mean, maybe, yes, eventually we might want to get married. But that's a very big if and—"

She cut him off. "But we don't have time to find out. I don't have anyplace else to live right now. Do you?"

"In a pinch, I could find a place." But not a good place, and she knew it.

"Where? Parked in your cousin's driveway? A sleeping bag on the floor at a friend's? And for how long? You don't have somewhere where you can study, let alone bring your children."

"I'm on the tribal housing list."

"I heard Steve Skillman say it takes years to get a house from the tribe. Don't forget, I know firsthand how hard it is to find a decent place to live here. You've told me yourself."

She was right. "Marriage is an extreme solution."

"Yes, it is," she agreed solemnly, "but if we got married, you could have everything you want. This place and, as quickly as possible, your kids. I would get to stay here. We could go on as we have. Marilyn Tall Feather wouldn't have to know the particulars of our arrangement. If I decide to leave at the end of the school year, I'll leave. You have your kids, you keep the house. You only gain.''

''What do you gain?''

''A good friend. A nice place to live. Blue, I'm not a romantic. I've had all that. It was wonderful, but it's over and it has been for a long time. I don't have to be in love with you to be a good partner for as long as it works for both of us.''

''What about me? Maybe I have to be in love.''

Shelley pulled her hand back, her expression shadowed in the failing light. ''Oh. I didn't even think. Are you in love with someone? Oh, Blue, I'm sorry. I thought you said you weren't involved with anyone now, and I just assumed—''

He was involved with a brown-haired, hazel-eyed woman who didn't seem to need love to marry. ''I'm not involved with someone else, and I'm not in love with someone else. But I think people should marry for love. Marriage is a commitment I take seriously. Even when I loved Carlene, it was hard enough.''

''Maybe it's harder when you love,'' Shelley said quietly.

Suddenly, he understood why she could offer marriage so easily. It was precisely because she didn't love him. If she did, she would be running away as fast as her little gray car would take her. Because if she loved, she would risk losing again.

He reached for her hand, took it back, enfolded it in both of his. Compassion flooded through him. Offering as much as she could give, she was responding to both their needs as best she could, and he knew without her telling him that she hadn't been this involved with anyone since her husband's death.

What's more, he knew marriage was probably the only way he could keep her in his life right now. It would be good for her, he thought. He was good for her. He could see that. She'd said as much. Could he give her a year and then let her walk away?

What was a year? Would he love her in a year? Would she love him? How might they hurt each other? It wouldn't be as neat and tidy as she seemed to think it would. Not for him, at any rate. And not for her, either, not if he had anything to say about it.

He let out a long breath. People married for worse reasons.

"I like sharing the house with you," he finally said. "We've been a good team this past week."

He felt her hand relax in his. "I think so, too."

"I've had girlfriends since Carlene and I split up, but nobody I wanted to marry. Nobody I didn't still feel lonely with." He rubbed a thumb over her knuckles. It was fully dark now, only the ghostly light from the security light in the yard limned Shelley's soft hair. Her eyes were obscured in shadow. "I don't feel lonely with you here, Shelley."

"Me, too. I mean…"

"I know what you mean. You already said it." He moved closer to her, leaning his head down to hers. "Let's get married, then."

Their faces were close, only a kiss apart. Their hands were still linked, nestled between their chests. Her eyes were solemn, colorless in the faint, silvered light. She nodded once.

Blue disengaged her hand and brought his arms around her shoulders. "Shelley?"

"Yes?"

"If we do this, I want a real marriage. For as long as it lasts."

She grew still in his arms, then dropped her gaze. "You mean sex."

"I mean lovemaking."

"I'd thought of that. I'm not sure I'm ready."

"I want to sleep with you. In the same bed. I want to wake up next to you in the morning, fall asleep snuggled close to you at night."

Her wide-eyed gaze bounced all over the room before returning to his face. "How do you know that so quickly?"

"Don't you know?"

She wasn't going to admit it if she did. "Blue, this is too fast."

That made him chuckle. "So getting married after knowing me a week is okay, but sleeping with me is more than you can handle. Seems to me most folks do that the other way around."

"But—"

He cut her off with a soft kiss. It took a few seconds before she relaxed into him, but she did, as he'd known she would. From the beginning, he'd known her body liked him, even if she wanted to keep him at a distance. If he married her, he had no intention of keeping his distance, and she might as well get used to it.

Trailing kisses along her jawline, he fitted his lips to her ear. "Shelley," he whispered, "I haven't had sex in over a year. I can go longer if I have to, but winters are long and cold here. If I live in this house with you, married or not, I'm going to want you. I can give you a little time to get used to the idea, but not forever. I'm only human."

"Blue." Her voice was thin. "I'm really not ready."

"How long has it been?" He knew, but he wanted her to say it, to start putting it in the past.

She tried to move out his embrace, but he only gave her a little distance, keeping his arms around her, his face close to hers.

"How long, Shelley?"

She could only shake her head, eyes downcast.

He shifted so they sat side by side, tucking her into his side, one arm around her shoulders, the other at her waist. She shuddered, and he knew she was fighting tears.

"Shh," he murmured against her hair. "It's okay."

They sat for a long time, long enough for the moon to rise behind them, flooding the room with silvery light and shadows.

Out of the silence, she finally spoke. "He was the only lover I've ever had."

Blue rocked her lightly, breathing in the fragrance of her hair. A tear splashed onto his forearm.

"Maybe it's time for a new lover, *cantesicela.*"

She sighed, relaxing a little against him. Her head fell into the hollow of his shoulder.

"We need each other," he continued, his voice low, soft, as gentle as he could make it. "Maybe it's only for this year, but we need each other."

"Maybe we do," she breathed.

He waited for her to say more. When she didn't, he asked, "Will you work on this with me?"

Shelley turned her face into his chest as if she were trying to hide.

"I'll try, Blue. I'll marry you, and I'll work on...a physical relationship. Just give me some time to get used to the idea."

He had some ideas about how he might help her do just that. "How about a month?"

Lifting her head, she couldn't hide the flash of panic in her eyes, but she agreed. "That's fair."

He wrapped his arms more tightly around her and laughed softly. "Then I guess we're engaged." He felt her smile against his neck. "You're sure this is what you want?"

"Everything will work out fine," she said.

It wasn't an answer to his question.

Then again, he wasn't sure he really wanted an answer.

March County High School looked much like hundreds of other American high schools. The small complex of plain brick buildings was located on the south side of Gilbert and included a gym, cafeteria, classrooms, a small library and administrative offices. It looked absolutely ordinary, but by three o'clock on Monday afternoon, Shelley felt as though she had slipped down Alice's rabbit hole into another world. In this world she was engaged to marry a thirty-six year old college senior. She taught Lakota students with lyrical names like Wanbli Kills in Water and Justin Her Many Horses in a school where Lakota drum music accompanied the morning announcements over the PA system, and where the first-day assembly featured Lakota prayers by tribal elders, the football team, cheerleaders and jingle dancers festooned with glittering metal and bright beadwork.

Somehow during the past week, even though she had sat through the Friday-morning orientation for new teachers, she hadn't comprehended how distinct Lakota culture was from the mainstream of American life. If she had made the mistake of believing countless news reports and newspaper features that implied that the defining characteristic of reservation life was rural poverty, she was quickly disabused of that notion. Lakota culture was far from dead, far from being a musty old relic of a glorious past. In the lives of her students and many of her colleagues, she could see it formed a rich background about which she knew next to nothing. She was also beginning to see how Lakota culture was an important part of Blue Larson, and she wanted to learn more about both him and his culture.

Shelley looked at the history textbook that lay open on her desk. It was a standard text, used across the country. There was little in the book that would connect with the experiences and history of her Lakota students.

"It's a bad sign when a new teacher looks so depressed at the end of the first day of school." An attractive Lakota woman stepped into her classroom, her long beaded earrings swinging as she walked forward. "I'm Jeanette Elk, the Lakota studies coordinator for the school district."

"You spoke at orientation last week." Shelley shook hands, recognizing her.

"Welcome to March County High. I hope you'll enjoy teaching here." Jeanette tipped her head in concern. "That was quite a frown. Is anything wrong?"

Shelley shook her head. "Not really. I've just realized that my textbook for this year is going to need a lot of supplementing. There's almost nothing in it about Native Americans, and even less about Lakota history. Since most of my students are Lakota, I think I'd better do something about that." She smiled at Jeanette. "So your timing is perfect."

Jeanette grinned. "You're a smart one. Whenever we get a new history teacher, I start working on them right away about those 'supplements.' I have lots of materials and resources on Lakota history you can use. My office is located at the back of the library."

"I'll stop by tomorrow during my prep period. I can see I need to do some studying. I don't know a thing about Lakota history or culture."

"Well, I've got a reading list I can give you, and the bookstore at the college has a good selection of all types of books about the Lakota and other tribes," Jeanette said.

"Why doesn't the school adopt texts that reflect more of the Lakota students' experiences?"

The older woman's eyes snapped briefly. "Long answer or short?"

"Whatever will help me serve these kids best."

Jeanette sat down in one of the desks in the front row. "The school board is made up mostly of white ranchers and their wives. Their kids go to school here, too, of course, but they don't always think Indian culture is that important. There are Lakota people who don't think Lakota language, culture or history should be taught in the schools, either. We have a long history of education being used against our culture, in the church schools and boarding schools in the past, nowadays in the public schools. Have you read anything about the boarding schools?"

Shelley shook her head. "I have a vague memory of something about students' mouths being washed out with soap for speaking their native languages."

"That happened to my mother," Jeanette told her. "And that was mild compared to some of what went on. Many people who are elders now had the Indian beat out of them. They were taught that everything Indian was wrong, that our language was bad, that our religion was devil worship, that our culture was backward. It takes time to turn around all those years of keeping Lakota ways out of schools.'' She smiled again. ''But we're getting there.''

''I'll need some help, but I'd like to incorporate more Lakota history into my classes.''

''I'm glad. I think you'll enjoy it.''

Shelley laughed. ''Probably more than my students will. If I could have stayed a student forever, I probably would have.''

''Why don't you take a Lakota studies class at the college?'' Jeanette suggested. ''They have some wonderful instructors, people who are really committed to helping the community. They'd be glad to have you.''

Blue strode through the back door of the room just then and joined the conversation. ''That's a great idea. I should have thought of that myself.'' He came to stand at Shelley's side. ''Hi, Jeanette. Giving Shelley some tips on Lakota history?''

Jeanette surveyed them with interest. ''Just letting her know what resources are available.''

It made Shelley nervous to have Blue there. She wasn't ready to tell people they were getting married. They were going to raise more than a few eyebrows.

Jeanette wasn't about to let them go without a question or two. ''Here for cross-country practice?''

Blue nodded. ''I should be home around five-thirty,'' he said to Shelley.

She blushed to the roots of her hair. That innocuous comment sounded so intimate, as if they were already married.

Jeanette cast them an arch look. ''You want to let me know what's going on so I can correct everybody else who gets it wrong?''

Blue exchanged a look with Shelley. ''Shell?''

All she could do was stare back at him.

He seemed to take her silence as acquiescence. "You know Melvin Heber was going to rent that little farmhouse west of town to me. Then Shelley showed up, and he gave it to her."

Jeanette made an impatient noise. "Big surprise."

"Yeah. Shelley offered to share the house. You know, roommates."

Jeanette laughed outright. "With you, Blue Larson? The best snag on the rez?" She grinned at Shelley. "Do you know how many women would commit a felony to be in your shoes?"

Shelley wanted the floor to swallow her up.

"Well," Blue continued, casually laying a hand on Shelley's back, "the roommate thing didn't work out quite the way we planned. We're getting married in a couple of weeks."

Goggle-eyed, Jeanette stared at them. "You're kidding."

"Nope." His smile seemed a little forced, but he stepped closer to Shelley, wrapping a protective arm around her. "That's the scoop, straight from the horse's mouth. Can you keep it close for a few hours? We just decided and we haven't told my mom yet. We're going up there after dinner tonight."

"You expect me to be quiet about this for more than a minute?"

"For my mom's sake only. I'll owe you one."

"You bet you will, Blue Larson. I don't know how I'm going to keep this to myself for a few minutes, never mind a few hours." She rose gracefully from the desk. "Congratulations. I think you've lost your mind, but I wish you the best."

Blue pressed a soft kiss to Shelley's temple. "Maybe I just lost my heart, not my mind."

Shelley tried her best to look happy, but her smile wobbled and she couldn't banish the pucker between her brows. Jeanette's assessing glance made her want to squirm. Blue said all the right things, but would anyone believe him?

"I'll leave you two alone, then. Geez." She drew the word out in a long, high-pitched syllable. "Brenda Sierra is going to be put out about this, I can tell you. And Emily Good Shield. And Tandra Bordeaux. And..." Jeanette walked out the door reciting women's names.

Shelley slumped against the desk. Blue pulled her up into his embrace.

"I'm sorry. I didn't think you'd be so upset." He rocked her once.

"I'm not upset. Just embarrassed."

He stilled. "Why?"

"It's like you said when we met. People will think I just came out here to find an Indian lover." She dropped her forehead onto his shoulder.

One of his hands came up to caress the back of her head. "They'll get over that once they get to know you. But you have to get used to telling people we're getting married."

"I know." She sighed. Then she laughed in spite of herself. "I've gotten so used to people feeling sorry for me. Now I have to get used to people thinking I'm crazy. I guess it's an improvement." She looked up at him.

He kissed her, one of his easy, comforting kisses. "Then you're okay?"

"I'm okay. See you in a couple of hours."

One more quick kiss, and he was gone.

Chapter Seven

Shelley stopped by the college and found a Lakota history course offered in the evening that she could attend. After registering, she visited the bookstore. In addition to course texts, there was a wide selection of books about and by Native Americans. She left with a bulging bag filled with the books for her class and a few others that had looked interesting, one on Lakota myth and another on healing ceremonies. The last was an impulse buy.

Over a simple supper of soup and salad, she and Blue planned their wedding. More accurately, Blue planned it. Shelley mostly nodded and said okay. He wanted to get blood tests done. It seemed prudent and it would lay to rest any fears she might have about health concerns. His cousin, Regina, and her husband, Toby, would be willing to stand up as witnesses at a simple civil ceremony. He'd called and gotten an appointment with a judge in Rapid City for a week from Friday. Could she take a personal day at work? He didn't have classes on Friday, and cross-country meets didn't start until the week after that. They could spend the weekend at a nice hotel in the Black Hills, where the aspens should be starting to turn. He wanted her to see the fall color in Spearfish Canyon.

When they left to go to his mother's, he opened the door of his truck for her.

"It's old, but it's clean," he said, helping her in. "After you meet my mom, I need to drop off some wood at my uncle's, if you don't mind."

She guessed she had to meet most of his family sooner of later. It was too small a community to avoid them. "That's fine. What's your mother like?"

The engine throbbed to life, and Blue backed up carefully. "She was raised down at Red Creek," he told her. "One of her uncles was a *wicasa wakan*. A medicine man. She grew up with the language and a lot of the old ways."

"What's that mean?" Shelley asked. "I really only realized today how little I know about Lakota ways. It all seems so different."

"Some of it is. You'll learn. My mom was raised real traditional, but she went to the boarding school at Wallace," he explained, referring to a town on the southern edge of the reservation. "The nuns and the priests were pretty harsh. She turned away from a lot of that old stuff. Met my dad, who was a mixed blood. Moved up to Lodgepole and raised her family there. Now she's going back to some of the Lakota ways again, but I didn't grow up with that."

"But what's she like? As a person?"

"She's quiet."

That wasn't encouraging.

"Is she going to be upset about…this?" She had trouble talking about their upcoming marriage. She needed to get past that.

"I don't think so." But he was frowning when she looked over at him. "She wants me to marry again."

"Not like this, though." Shelley looked back out the window at the rolling grasslands.

"Well, we don't have to tell her everything."

"What if she asks?"

"She won't. She'll watch and draw her own conclusions." He reached across the bench seat to briefly put a hand on hers. "It'll be fine. When are you going to tell your parents?" He stopped at the junction with the state highway that went north to Lodgepole, then pulled smoothly onto the blacktop.

Shelley looked out at the highway. "I don't know."

"Are you planning on telling them at all?" His voice was cool.

"I'm afraid they'll be worried if I do. They'll think I've gone off the deep end. I wouldn't put it past my mother to come out here as soon as she hears."

"Did you tell them about me at all?"

"Yeah. On the phone last night."

"What'd you say? How'd they respond?"

"I said I had a roommate. A student at the tribal college."

"You didn't tell them your roommate was a man, did you?"

She huffed a little. "Not in so many words."

"Chicken."

He was right about that. "Afraid so."

"What are you so afraid of?"

"That…" She'd started to say that they'd think she was crazy. But with her parents, it wasn't that simple.

"That they'll think you shouldn't move on with your

life, find another husband?" Blue supplied, with a little more insight than she liked.

"Partly," she admitted. "And that I might be doing something rash."

"Like entering into a marriage of convenience?"

She cast him an irritated look. "Yes."

"I think you should tell them."

She decided then and there that she would tell her parents when *she* was good and ready and not a moment sooner. "I'm going to wait."

They rode in silence for several minutes, then slowed as they entered the small town that housed the tribal headquarters. Turtle Creek ran through the center of the town, and houses lay scattered through the valley and up and down the draws and hills that flanked it.

Blue turned onto a street running up a steep hill a little too quickly, throwing a spray of gravel into the ditch. "Fine, don't tell your parents you're getting married," he said tersely. "But it's going to be awkward to call them in six months and say, oh, by the way, I've been married since September. Thought you might like to know."

"What difference does it make to you?" Shelley retorted sharply, surprised by his pique.

"No difference. No difference at all. This is where my mom lives." He changed the subject abruptly as they pulled into the parking lot of a small senior-citizens housing complex. The pickup lurched to a halt. "Let's go."

Blue had to force himself to calm down as he guided Shelley to his mother's door. It really wasn't any of his business if she didn't want to tell her parents they were getting married. He was acting as if they were entering into a real marriage, for the usual reasons. He knew better. What was wrong with him?

As he glanced at her beside him, he was struck again with how pretty she was and how fragile. His anger dissipated, replaced by the desire to make her smile. He was irritated, he realized, because he knew she was thinking she might never have to tell her parents she'd married him. She was thinking she might be long gone a year from now, their little arrangement a mere footnote in her adventure on the rez, nothing worth mentioning to the most important people in her life.

He rapped on his mother's door, noticing that that didn't sit well with him at all.

Irritated or not, Shelley edged closer to Blue when the door swung open to reveal a short, heavy woman in a plain cotton housedress, her graying hair tucked into a bun. Despite her roundness, her features suggested strength and resolve, with penetrating dark eyes set at an exotic slant above high cheekbones. She only glanced at them before turning into her living room, leaving the door open.

"Hi, Ma," Blue said, motioning for Shelley to go ahead.

"Shut the door," was Mrs. Larson's response. "You want coffee?"

"In a minute, Ma," he said, calling her back from the kitchen of the small one-bedroom apartment. "I'd like you to meet someone first."

The older woman turned slowly to face them. Her expression didn't shift a bit as she clasped her hands over her middle.

"Mom, I'd like to introduce you to Shelley Mathews. She teaches history at the high school. Shelley, this is my mother, Eloise Larson."

Mrs. Larson dipped her head briefly in acknowledgment.

"It's a pleasure to meet you, Mrs. Larson," Shelley said, her voice much smaller than she would have liked.

Blue went on. "Shelley and I are getting married a week from Friday."

Silence stretched out for long moments, running into more than a minute while Blue's mother simply looked at Shelley. Shelley met her gaze, wishing she had some idea what to say. Nothing came to her. Not one thing.

At last Blue's mother shifted her gaze to him. "I got a blackberry pie," she said. "You want some?"

The tension eased. Blue smiled. "You bet I do."

"Can I help you with anything?" Shelley asked.

Mrs. Larson waved one hand. "Sit."

They sat.

The visit with Blue's mother was awkward. The coffee and the pie were excellent, but the conversation was decidedly one-sided. Blue did almost all the talking, telling his mother how he and Shelley had met.

Eloise Larson looked unimpressed. "Bet this marriage helps you get your kids faster," she observed when he was done.

"It might," Blue said.

Blue gave an outline of Shelley's background, leaving out any mention of Brad or his death. Mrs. Larson's eyes never left her as Blue talked.

When he finished, she sat in silence, still watching Shelley.

"You been married before?"

Shelley hesitated.

When Blue started to answer for her, his mother hushed him. "She can talk."

"Yes. My husband died four years ago."

Eloise nodded curtly. "You got to let him go."

How did she know? Looking into her dark eyes, Shelley knew that she did.

"You're going to have a new husband. My son."

Shelley looked at Blue. "Yes."

"It's no good to have two husbands, especially if one of them's a ghost."

Turning her gaze to her future mother-in-law, Shelley tried to reassure her. "It's been a long time," she said. "It's in the past."

"Not yet." Eloise nodded at Blue. "Take her out to Verdell's. Have her sweat before the wedding. It'll help."

Blue nodded. "Okay."

The older woman clicked her tongue. "You should wait."

Neither Blue nor Shelley said anything.

They left his mother's shortly afterward to drop off the firewood at Blue's uncle's house. Shelley endured another round of introductions and startled reactions to the news of their impending marriage, but Blue's Uncle Jim—his mother's brother—and Jim's family, while surprised, were a more forgiving audience.

Shelley wasn't certain of all the relationships, but two young women who appeared to be Blue's cousins tittered and teased Blue until he begged them to stop. Aunt Janiece patted Shelley's arm and told her not to let Eloise get to her. Blue's mother had her own ways, Janiece claimed, but she was a good woman. All you had to do was look at Blue for proof of that. Shelley still wished she had been easier to talk to.

"Your mother knows exactly why we're getting married," Shelley said to Blue once they were on the way home.

"Looks like it," Blue agreed. "But I don't think she's

too worried about it. She'd have called Janiece right away if she had been.''

"I don't think she liked me."

"I don't think she's made a decision yet."

"Blue, how did she know about Brad?"

He shrugged. "She's pretty observant. Intuition. Sometimes she just knows things."

"It made me uncomfortable. What else does she know?"

"Don't worry about it."

"Is she a medicine woman?"

Blue didn't laugh, as she'd thought he might. "Not exactly. But she has power."

That wasn't a particularly comforting answer. "What kind of power?"

"She knows things sometimes. She understands things about people without them having to tell her. She's seventy-two years old, Shelley. She's seen a lot. She's wise. Maybe *wisdom* is a better word for what she has than *power*."

"She knew about Brad. That's more than wisdom."

"Maybe not. Maybe she could see how sad you are and just figured it out."

"I'm not sad."

He glanced over at her, the lights from the dash casting a faint glow over his face. "You have shadows in your eyes."

Would they ever go away? "I don't feel so sad anymore," she insisted.

He made an indeterminate sound.

"What did your mother mean when she said you should take me to Verdell's to sweat?" she asked.

"Verdell Owens is one of the Lakota studies instructors at the college. He and his wife have a sweat lodge out at their place, down by Wallace. The sweat is a ceremony. There are prayers. It's for purification."

"I've heard of the sweat lodge. How does it work?"

"Stones are heated in a fire, then put inside a small lodge made of a willow frame covered with blankets. When the door closes, the prayers begin and cedar and other herbs are thrown onto the rocks. Then water is poured onto them to make steam."

"Like a sauna?"

"Like a sauna that cleanses the spirit, as well as the body. I'd like to take you out to meet the Owenses. You don't have to sweat if you don't want to."

"It sounds interesting."

"It's a good thing to do. I think Verdell's having a sweat Saturday. We could go down, meet some people, even if you decide not to sweat."

"All right. Why does your mother think it would help me?"

"It helps everyone."

Shelley was quiet as they turned onto the section road that led back to their house. When they reached the driveway, she turned to look at Blue.

"I haven't thought about Brad so much since I've been here," she told him, needing to counter his mother's comments somehow. "It's getting easier."

Blue pulled the truck to a stop near the house, then looked at her. "Traditionally, Lakota people don't say the names of the dead out loud. It's said to call them back. Make it hard for them to go on."

She felt chastised. "Do you believe that?"

Once again, he shrugged his shoulders. "I don't know."

"I won't ever forget him."

"I didn't say you should."

"Your mother did."

"No. She said you had to let him go. It's not the same thing."

Shelley knew he was right.

She also knew that she had more to let go of than Brad. An image formed in her mind, an image of a boy's face, tearstained, an expression of regret and sorrow contorting his features. She felt no compassion for him, not the smallest amount.

All she felt was anger: hot, virulent, seething. The boy had good reason to cry. In one stupid, foolish moment, he'd changed so many lives forever. Hers. Brad's. The family they might have had together. Brad's parents' and sisters'. Nothing could ever be the same again. All her dreams, all her love, stolen in the second it had taken to pull the trigger of a gun.

She opened the door. "I'll be in in a little while," she said, her voice belying her agitation, she knew. "I need a few minutes by myself."

Blue left her.

Alone, Shelley walked to the edge of the field in front of the house, surprised by the strength of the anger coursing through her.

Letting go. So easy to say. So obvious. And she'd tried. She'd seen therapists, gone to support groups. None of it helped. She still hated that boy, hated what he'd done.

She'd thought it would be better, leaving San Diego, coming to a new place, and it had been—until tonight. Here it was again, this consuming anger, making her heart pound, her muscles twitch, her hands close into hard fists. If anything, it was worse than it had been for a long time. She'd been able to drown the anger by tuning out everything, but it wasn't working as well anymore.

Instead, her eyes were drowning in hot tears. Angry tears. Furious tears.

Why was she out here in this empty, open country so far from the ocean and the deserts she had loved? What was she doing living in an old farmhouse in the middle of an Indian reservation? What in heaven's name was she doing planning to marry a man she'd known for a little more than a week? This wasn't the life she was supposed to have. This wasn't *her* life anymore. It belonged to a stranger, someone else. Not her.

The only thing that felt like it was hers right now was her hatred, her resentment, her anger. And her memories of Brad, the memories of who she had been, what her life had been like before that wretched boy had killed her husband and the life they had shared. The memories were all she had left.

If she let it go, if she let Brad go, who would she be?

Shelley looked to the sky as if in search of a response, but the bright stars kept their own counsel, offering no answers, until they were swallowed up by clouds streaming in on the west wind. By the time the last star faded from view, Shelley imagined herself wrapped in the clouds, cushioned from the pain, hidden in the darkening sky. The anger slowly leeched from her, following the wind.

If she found no answers, it no longer mattered.

Nothing mattered now, because once more, she felt nothing.

Bethany Garreaux, the tenth-grade cross-country star, made quite an entrance the day she finally decided to show up to her third-period history class. Ten minutes into the lesson, the door burst open and a beautiful, long-legged girl with short, wispy dark hair and huge almond eyes, all mock innocence, tumbled into the room. Every eye in the class was on her.

"Hi! Is this sophomore history? Sorry I'm late. It happens." The girl's voice was bright, her smile full of challenge.

The students waited for Shelley to respond to the interruption.

She knew immediately who the girl was. Bethany's haircut had been the talk of the tenth grade all week. In a school where most girls had long hair and carefully gelled bangs, Bethany's trendy cut stood out. Dressed as she was in a short skirt and a cutoff top that bared her midriff and played hide-and-seek with her well-developed curves, Bethany Garreaux epitomized the kind of casual beauty most teenagers could only fantasize about.

"Good morning, Bethany. Please sit down. I'll bring you up-to-date after class." Shelley resumed her lesson. "George, you were about to share your group's research questions for the first unit...?"

Bethany wasn't ready to be dismissed so summarily. "I see my reputation gets around," she said to Shelley, completely ignoring George as she flounced into an empty seat near the door. "I know your name, too, Ms. Mathews. Or should I say Mrs. Larson?"

Chapter Eight

Shelley hadn't said anything to her classes about her impending marriage, though she knew some of the students had to have heard about it.

Bethany chattered on, playing her audience for all it was worth. "I have to say, I'm impressed. You've been here how long? A couple of weeks? That's pretty fast work, Ms. Mathews-Larson. And Mr. Larson is a babe."

Snickers, chuckles and hoots erupted from the class.

"That's enough, Bethany." Shelley maintained a cool, slightly amused facade. "'Ms. Mathews' will do fine. Now, let's get back to work. George, you were about to say…?"

Shelley kept a pleasant smile fixed on Bethany, expecting her to claim the floor again at any moment. George explained the questions his group wanted to explore regarding the motivations of the early settlers in the New World and how their values and beliefs affected their relationships with the Native Americans they encountered. When he finished, Bethany broke in again.

"You mean we have to figure this out on our own? Aren't you supposed to tell us this stuff?" she asked in a peeved voice. "That's your job, isn't it?"

Shelley sent her a bland look. "You'd prefer to sit through a fifty-minute lecture every day?"

"Sure. Gives me a chance to catch up on my reading." She flashed a copy of a popular comic series.

Titters sounded throughout the class as students tried to suppress their amusement.

Shelley played along with an exaggerated grin. "It's always a pleasure to see students who like to read on their own." She turned back to the class. "Now, Group Three, Mrs. Jackson is expecting you in the library. Go on ahead. The other groups can spend the rest of the period preparing your presentations for next week."

Students began moving around, shifting desks into working circles, sharing papers and books. Shelley took the seat next to Bethany. Up close, she caught a glimpse of fading bruises on the girl's underarm. When Bethany saw the direction of Shelley's gaze, she shifted her shoulder so her arm was at a different angle, hiding the bruises.

Shelley had seen bruises like that before on students, the small, half-moon impressions where long fingernails had dug into tender flesh.

Teachers were required to report suspected abuse.

Schooling her expression into a pleasant mask, Shelley looked more carefully at Bethany. Skillfully applied makeup at her collarbone concealed more bruising, but these marks were of a different nature. Shelley suspected an enthusiastic boyfriend, another bad sign.

"You're in Group Four, Bethany," she said softly.

"Kelly and Adam can help explain what they're doing, but I'll need to see you after class, as well."

"I hate history," Bethany snapped. "I'm not going to be living in the past, you know. Why don't we have future studies or something relevant instead of all this dumb old stuff?"

Shelley had to smile. "That's an interesting question. It might make a good research project someday."

Bethany groaned. "You love this stuff, don't you?"

Shelley nodded. "I'm afraid so."

"Figures." Bethany slumped in her seat. "What's the attraction of living in the past?"

"I don't live in the past, Bethany, I study it." A voice inside her head mocked her. Liar, it said. You do, too, live in the past. Shelley ignored it. "I like the sense of connection history gives me. It's exciting to look around and see ideas, buildings, nations, even businesses that have grown out of the accumulated experience of people through time."

Bethany rolled her eyes. "Gag. Boring. I want to move forward. Never look back. I can't wait to get out of this place. Nothing good ever happened here, and it never will. Not for me, anyway."

Whether she meant the school or the community or both, it disturbed Shelley to hear such a bleak assessment from a fifteen-year-old.

They looked at each other for a long moment. Bethany, one eyebrow raised, her lip curved in mocking expectation, was clearly prepared to challenge any response Shelley might make.

"I'm sorry things are so difficult." Her voice was very low, as matter-of-fact as Bethany's had been, without pity.

Momentarily disarmed, Bethany's eyes dropped to her desktop.

Shelley didn't give her a chance to reply. "Well, why don't you join your group now? We'll talk again after class."

After dinner that evening, Shelley took a folding chair out into the yard to enjoy the sunset while she read the first batch of papers her students had turned in. Blue was studying inside, and Shoonk dozed at her side. She got up once to get a sweater, the slight chill in the air heralding the coming of autumn.

When the sun sat poised on the horizon, Blue came out, chair in hand, to join her. He sat close enough to lean his shoulder against hers, and the warmth of his body felt good.

"Bethany finally showed up at school today," he said.

"Yes, we met. She's quite something." She told him about Bethany's grand entrance. "She's difficult. One of those kids who instinctively knows how to push buttons. She told everyone you were a babe."

Blue chuckled. "She told me at practice this afternoon that she was going to flunk history this year."

"If she doesn't come to class or do her work, she might," Shelley observed.

"She's got to get her grades up to a *C* this quarter if she wants to stay on the team. I know her life is tough, but I can't let her run if she doesn't have the grades."

"She's certainly bright enough."

The sun had slipped halfway below the edge of the prairie.

Blue shifted so that he pressed a little more closely against her side. "She didn't come earlier this week because her mom came back from a couple days of being wasted and didn't want her to leave.''

Shelley had had students with alcoholic and drug-addicted parents before. ''So Bethany stays to take care of her, and her schooling suffers.''

''More than her schooling.''

''She has bruises.''

He nodded.

''Has anyone reported it?''

''Yeah. Social services and the tribe both know. Bethany was in a foster home for a while the year before last. It didn't work out. Her mom went to rehab for a while, so they sent Bethany back.''

''I have to make a report again.''

The sun disappeared in a molten blaze of gold and red. Blue tucked his arm around her. ''It probably won't change anything.''

Shelley could tell that upset him. ''I don't have a choice. It's the law. She didn't like me very well as it is. This will probably make her hate me.''

''Give her a chance, Shell. She's only a kid underneath that sophisticated exterior.''

''I know. She'll have every chance I'd give any of my students.''

Shelley felt herself torn between caring about what happened to Bethany Garreaux and the familiar, more comfortable distance she'd maintained from her students since Brad's death. Had she been different before? She couldn't even remember anymore, but she was always fair with her students, even if she preferred to remain aloof. She would give Bethany every opportunity to do well in her class.

Why, then, was she feeling more attached to this girl than she usually did? Especially considering the way

Bethany had behaved in class, it surprised her. Besides, she knew there were limits to what a teacher could do. Caring a great deal didn't necessarily mean she would be able to help Bethany any better.

Blue leaned close to drop a kiss just below her ear. "What are you thinking about?"

"Nothing."

His breath was warm on her skin. His lips covered hers in one of his gentle kisses. "Can I lure you back inside for a dish of ice cream?"

He made her smile so easily sometimes. "That you could." She gathered up her papers, and Blue carried the chairs back in for the night.

As soon as she set foot in the school the next morning, Shelley knew something was wrong. There was an unnatural hush in the halls as students milled about. She saw one girl holding another who appeared to be crying in her arms.

In the office, Jeanette Elk was talking quietly with Linda Lee Gesler, the school secretary.

"Good morning," Shelley greeted the women as she picked up the announcements in her box. "What happened?"

"Three of our students were in a car accident late last night. One of them, Eddie Sight, didn't make it. Two others are in critical condition. They were airlifted to McKinnon Hospital in Sioux Falls," Jeanette told her.

Shelley recognized the boy's name from the assembly on Monday. He'd been a member of the football team, a tall, good-looking senior. Now he was dead.

Just like that.

Her heart pounded rapidly, and she took a deep breath, quelling the urge to turn around and walk out.

"What happened?" She knew the school would be buzzing with rumors. It was best to get all the information straight at the beginning.

"Their car stalled on the highway, and they were hit by a drunk driver before they could get off the road. The tribal police and a grief counselor will be here for an assembly third period to talk to the kids." Jeanette wiped a tear from the corner of her eye.

Linda Lee spoke up. "Eddie's cousin, Stanley, is in the tenth grade. He's in your last-period class, but he probably won't be in for a few days."

"Of course." Another student who would need a little extra time and attention. "Thank you for letting me know. Will you excuse me?"

Shelley walked slowly down the corridor, focusing on each footstep, one after the other, noting the click of her heels on the freshly waxed floors, pushing anger away from her with every step toward her classroom. Build the wall, she told herself. Wall off the feelings. Push them back.

Shelley stopped suddenly. What had she just told herself? Build the wall. Wall off the anger, the feelings.

Dear God, she thought. What am I doing? Was this how she handled everything now? Build a wall. Create distance. Step back. Hide.

Yes, she realized. This *was* how she handled everything now. She built walls. She ran away to a safe place inside herself where she didn't feel anything bad because she didn't feel anything at all.

She walked into her room and closed the door behind her, leaning back against it. Today, with this tragedy, she didn't know the boy who had been killed or those who had been so badly hurt. She had automatically slid into the pain and anger she'd been holding on to for so long. It had come up on Monday night, and here it was again.

Shelley knew for certain that she didn't like how the anger—no, rage—felt one bit better than she had when Brad had first been killed. She also knew she was going to have to deal with it finally, or find a way to permanently wall it off.

The idea of dealing with it made her want to cry.

Might there be a way to permanently wall off the pain and anger? She knew that wasn't a healthy thought, but it still tempted her.

If there was a way to permanently wall off the pain and anger, Shelley didn't find it that Friday. The day was emotionally exhausting, and a waste of academic time because the students were too upset to work productively. It seemed everyone knew the boys involved in the accident, and many were related to them. By the last period of the day, Shelley simply let them talk quietly among themselves while she circulated, listening.

"I talked to Stanley this morning," Brendan Wilke said. "He says his grandmother's going to keep the ghost."

"My auntie did that when my cousin died," added Pete Good Shield.

Shelley's ears pricked up. "What's that mean, Brendan? To keep a ghost?"

"It's one of the old ceremonies. Indian religion," he said. "When somebody dies, they don't always want to let his spirit go right away. They want to help him on the spirit path. They make a special place for the ghost and feed him and take care of him for a while. Then there's a ceremony and a giveaway and they let him go."

Shelley felt a shiver run down her spine.

"It helps people get through their loss," he said with

far more wisdom than Shelley thought a tenth-grader should have had.

"It helped my aunt a lot," Pete stated.

Shelley moved on to the next group of students without saying anything more.

The first Saturday in September dawned bright and clear and as hot as a blacksmith's forge. By noon, the towering anvils of approaching thunderstorms ranged across the western sky. By three o'clock, the fierce winds and tornado warnings had reached March County. Blue reluctantly called Verdell Owens to tell him he and Shelley wouldn't make it to the sweat.

He found Shelley out in the yard, staring up at the churning clouds.

"Better put your car in." He handed her the keys, and followed. "If you pull all the way to the right, I can get my truck in, too."

By the time the cars were in the shed, the sky had turned a sickly greenish gray.

"What do we do if there's a tornado?" Shelley asked.

"Head for the basement and pray. The warning sirens will go off in town. We'll be able to hear them."

They stood together looking up at the swirling sky. The old elms swayed, creaking in the wind. Several dead branches had fallen.

"It's kind of exciting," Shelley said. "We don't have this kind of storm in San Diego."

About a mile to the west, where the section road met the highway, the sky descended to meet the ground in an impenetrable gray veil. Small hailstones began to ping on the corrugated-metal roof of the car shed.

"Time to go inside." Blue grabbed her hand and ran for the house. Shoonk was on the porch waiting for them.

He barked when they paused to watch the hail advance from the shelter of the porch. Blue let Shoonk inside, then drew a protective arm around Shelley, holding the door open.

The temperature dropped ten degrees in less than a minute and the hail clattered on the roof, shredded the leaves on the trees and bounced wildly on the grass. In a few moments, the yard was white, covered with ice. Shelley reached out a hand to catch a hailstone, then snatched it back before Blue could warn her.

"Ouch!" She brought her hand to her mouth. "It stings. I can see how it would damage cars."

Blue took her hand and placed a kiss on a small red mark. "And this is just the little stuff," he said.

She watched the hail beat down the hollyhocks along a section of fence where there were no trees to shelter them. "It's so destructive."

"That's the power of the thunderbirds," Blue said.

The wind gusted, bringing heavy, splashing rain that blew up onto the porch. In only a few seconds, they were both soaked. Blue bundled Shelley through the door and pulled it tight behind them.

"I'd say we outstayed our welcome." He flipped his sopping hair back out of his eyes. Then he caught sight of Shelley watching him.

The front of her hair and clothes were wet, her thin knit shirt hugging every curve of her torso. She was chilled, and her nipples stood out clearly.

Without thinking, he reached for her.

Chapter Nine

Shelley's cheeks were cool and damp from the rain, but her mouth warmed rapidly beneath his. The faraway air she'd had yesterday and most of today had vanished with the storm. Now, in his arms, there was only the kiss and the elemental attraction between them.

Lightning flashed outside, followed quickly by cracking thunder. Neither one of them flinched. Blue maneuvered Shelley into the living room, backing her up until the wall was at her back. He pinned her hips with his, and his fingers found the hem of her shirt. Up and under they delved, seeking skin and heat.

He rained kisses on her face all the while, collecting any lingering raindrops with his tongue. He sipped from her chin, her cheeks, her eyebrows, her temples. She tasted sweeter than September plums, and as her skin began to heat, he could scent her arousal. With a growl, he returned to her mouth, demanding entrance as his hand claimed her breast.

Rational thought fled. All there was in his universe was Shelley, her firm nipple growing harder between his fingers, her tongue soft and teasing in an intimate dance with his. Even the sounds of the storm raging outside receded as he lost himself in her. He rolled his hips against hers, seeking the juncture of her thighs. He found it, pressed himself into her. Without thought, his hips and his tongue established a pulsing rhythm that set him on fire. He wanted her as he'd never wanted any woman.

He pushed her shirt up, anxious to get the wet material away from the silky skin he wanted to see, then kiss. He broke the kiss to pull the shirt over her head.

Shelley's eyes flew open when he did. As the shirt cleared her head, she snatched it back before her, thrusting it and her hands against his chest, pushing him back.

"Stop," she gasped.

He rocked his hips into her once more, unable to control the movement, his body screaming for completion.

She stood against the wall, blinking, head lowered.

"I'm not going to apologize." His voice was ragged.

"No, of course not."

"I want you, Shelley."

She looked at him, but shadows claimed her eyes. Somewhere, deep inside herself, she was burying what she had felt only a moment before. Blue watched her retreat, frustrated, angry that she could turn away from her own passion this way, angry that she could turn away from him.

He caught her wrists, still wrapped inside her shirt. "Where do you go when you do that?"

Feeling flashed briefly, only to be quickly shuttered. "What do you mean?"

"I don't want you to shut me out," he said with quiet control. He wanted to shake her, to shake loose the feelings she was so ruthlessly quelling.

She frowned, looking more baffled than anything. "You make me feel things," she whispered.

"What's so wrong with that?"

She only stared at him.

"Shelley, why don't you want to feel the passion between us?"

"Because it makes me feel other things, too. Things I don't want to feel." She wrenched away from him and fled to the doorway to her room, only a few feet away. She stopped there, her bare skin pebbled now with gooseflesh. She made no move to cover herself. "I'm not ready yet, Blue."

He caught her arm again, not wanting to let her close the door between them, then letting her go immediately, knowing that he had to. "Are you ever going to be?"

She walked into her room, out of his line of vision. "I don't know."

The door clicked softly shut.

The night before her wedding, Shelley sat on the edge of her turned-down bed, staring at a framed photograph cradled in her hands. In the picture, a young woman in a wedding dress smiled at a tall, reed-slender young man with blond hair and laughing eyes. His tuxedo made him look even younger than he had been.

It had been June, and she had been twenty-one, just out of college, ready to begin graduate school and life as a married woman. The happy girl in the photograph had been so full of hopes and dreams. She and Brad had planned their entire lives together. Her teaching credential, then medical school for him. Then they would buy a house and start a family. In the plans these newlyweds had made, their first child would have been born two years ago. By now, a second might be on the way. They had wanted three.

Shelley sighed. Tomorrow afternoon she was going to marry again. This time there were no hopes, no dreams, no plans.

A soft knock sounded on her door.

"Yes?"

Blue had never come into her bedroom, but he pushed open the door and stepped inside. He had given her a lot of room since last Saturday's storm. It surprised her that she didn't really mind him here in her private space.

"Can I come in?"

She set the photograph facedown on the small table beside the bed. "Yes, of course."

He came to the side of the bed and pulled the covers back, motioning for her to tuck her legs under.

She hesitated.

"Don't worry, I won't climb in with you. I'm not here to try to seduce you." His smile was gentle.

Shelley slipped her legs under the covers and sat back against the pillows as he covered her. Blue sat down beside her, leaning one hand across her to rest on the bed. The other opened to reveal a small box wrapped in white paper tied with a blue ribbon.

"I have something I wanted to give you tonight."

Shelley searched his face before accepting the tiny box. "You shouldn't have. I didn't..."

He put a finger to her lips. "Shh. Just open it."

Inside was a ring unlike any she had ever seen. It was a wide silver band inlaid with tiny, exquisitely crafted running horses in colored stone, black and green and a glowing reddish brown.

"It's beautiful," she breathed.

"The horses reminded me of you." He took the ring and placed it on the ring finger of her right hand. "They're beautiful animals. They survive in the wild by developing a finely honed sense of flight. It takes patience and persistence to get a wild horse to trust you, but it's worth the effort."

She turned her hand to admire the ring in the light from the bedside lamp. "So I'm a wild horse, am I?"

He caught her hand and brought it to his lips. "You're beautiful," he said, evading her question with a smile.

"You just said I was a horse."

"You *remind* me of a wild horse. You—" he felt for her waist through the bedclothes and bounced her in a teasing fashion "—appear to be very much of a woman."

Their eyes met, and he let her go.

"Thank you, Blue. It's a beautiful gift."

"You're welcome." He reached over to pick up the photograph from the table. She started to reach for it, then let him take it.

He studied it in silence, then replaced it on the table, this time standing up so it was visible.

"We don't have to do this," he said.

"I know. I don't mind."

Small furrows appeared between his brows. "Maybe that's what bothers me."

"Why?"

"It seems like you ought to care at least a little bit."

She put her hand to his cheek, smoothed back his hair. "We've talked about this before. Have you changed your mind?"

It took him a long time to answer, so long Shelley thought he might have changed his mind.

"No." His voice was firm. "I haven't changed my

mind." He folded her hands between his and raised them for a chaste kiss. "Good night, *cantesicela.*"

"What's that mean?"

"'Sad heart.'" He tapped his index finger on each of her eyebrows. "Maybe someday I'll see your heart smile again."

When he left her, Shelley felt oddly better. This marriage was entirely different from her first. It was a marriage for all the wrong reasons. Yet Blue Larson was a good man—a very good man—she thought, looking at the ring on her hand.

A tiny stirring of hope unfurled in her breast. For what, she could not say, but she was grateful for it as she slipped toward sleep.

The next day, Friday, the air was crisp and cool as summer waned in the Black Hills and the plains surrounding them. The wedding ceremony in Rapid City was a simple civil affair. Shelley wore an Indian printed skirt and blouse. Blue wore a dark suit, but Regina and Toby were in jeans. Their kids waited in their van, reading comic books in anticipation of a day at the mall and the movies. In some respects, it hardly seemed like a wedding to Shelley.

And it wasn't a real wedding, after all. Yet when Blue took her hand to slip a simple gold wedding band onto the third finger of her left hand, Shelley looked into his eyes and felt emotions she struggled to name. Blue was fast becoming one of the best friends she had ever had. His friendship touched her deeply, and he was so handsome, so generous. He was more than a good man, she realized. He was among the best.

The suggestion of hope she had felt the night before grew when the judge pronounced them husband and wife.

"You may kiss the bride," he directed, and Shelley smiled.

Blue took her in his arms. "You looked pleased," he said, and there was a satisfied light in his eyes when he kissed her.

Shelley kissed him back.

She had only been married a moment, and if she was pleased, she was also confused. This was a marriage of convenience. More than anything, Shelley valued her friendship with Blue. He gave freely, and he would give more if she would accept it. Blue was ready to be her husband. Was she ready to be his wife?

Outside the courthouse, Blue and Shelley shook hands with Regina and Toby, who left immediately, then walked slowly to the car. Blue opened the door of the car for her, then went around to the driver's side. Neither of them said a word as he drove through town to the interstate.

Shelley looked out the windows as they drove west and north. She knew Blue had reservations at one of the newly restored hotels in Deadwood, the local gambling mecca in the heart of the Black Hills. She hadn't asked him to get two rooms, and wondered if he had. She'd promised him a physical relationship, and really, she didn't know why she was having such a hard time with it. She was attracted to him, unquestionably. All she had to do was stop thinking and let her body take over. It was that simple.

It *should* have been that simple.

But it wasn't.

Maybe she wanted to be in love, after all. That, however, would mean opening the door to feelings she didn't want. The past couple of weeks had made that clear.

The scenery rolled past as they drove through a wide

valley, dark mountains on the left, a last, outlying ridge of hills on the right, with views of the plains beyond peeking through the gaps.

The only simple truth in her life right now was that Shelley didn't know what she wanted. So much had changed. So much was changing.

They exited at Sturgis and drove down a long, tree-lined street that ended at a junction with Highway 34. Deadwood was to the left, the sign said. Blue turned right. Shelley didn't ask why, and he didn't say.

A mile or two past the turn, the highway broke through the last line of hills onto the open plains. A solitary mountain loomed a short distance to the north. Shelley watched it grow closer as Blue turned at another junction and drove straight for the mountain.

Neither of them said a word when he turned onto the road posted with a sign identifying Bear Butte State Park. Up and down the swells of the rising mountain meadows they rode. A handful of buffalo grazed in a pasture. A meadowlark sang jubilantly, invisible in the grassy hillocks. They passed an A-frame headquarters building and mounted a sweeping curve of narrow road, then found themselves in an empty parking lot.

Blue got out to open her door, helped her out and took her hand as he walked to the edge of the asphalt. A wide meadow dropped away below them, rising on the far side to pale, rocky cliffs and spires. To the left, the main mass of the mountain rose in twin humps, the Ponderosa pines cutting dark lines down the reddish talus slopes. High clouds streaked the sky with milky ribbons, and the air held a cool clarity that caught Shelley's attention in an odd way. It made her listen closely, though for what, she wasn't sure.

"This is Bear Butte," Blue said, his voice hushed. "It's a holy place."

High above the cliffs, a hawk wheeled and drifted toward them. Shelley waited for Blue to continue.

"There's a short hike, about a mile or so, that goes up that draw—" he pointed with a bob of his chin "—then circles back across the face of that slope and down that trail there." He indicated the trailhead beside a large map and information billboard. "Would you like to come? Our walking shoes are in the trunk."

"Yes, I'd like that." She watched the hawk glide back toward the cliffs. "I've read about Bear Butte for my class at the college. I didn't realize it was this close to the Black Hills."

Blue rummaged through his bag and pulled out a pair of jeans and a rugby shirt along with his athletic shoes. "That's right—I forgot you'd know all about the history."

"Not yet. I've only started learning." She opened the zipper of her small bag and found her shoes and jeans.

"Crazy Horse and Sitting Bull were here. Fools Crow came here, too. People come now to pray and cry for visions. This has been one of the most important places for the Lakota since ancient times. For other tribes, too."

"It feels..." She lifted her head, searching the mountain, trying to define what she felt here. "It feels alive," she decided. "Like there's someone else here, someone we can't see."

Blue didn't laugh, as she'd thought he might. "There's a lot of power here," he said. "Shelley, I..." Now it was his turn to hesitate. "I came here today to pray."

"Oh." That surprised her. She didn't think of him as religious. "Would you rather go alone?"

"No." He waited for her to look at him. "I'd like you

to come, but I won't ask you to say or do anything. But we were married today. For as long as it lasts, I'd like to ask for blessings on our marriage, and to give thanks. I'd like you with me.''

"Give thanks for what?" Too late, she realized she was prying.

"For you," he said simply. "That you would do this to help me get my kids back sooner."

She didn't know what to say.

"But also, just for you."

The naked honesty of his simple sentiment left her speechless. She wanted to deny it, to turn away, but the warmth in his dark eyes held her silent, watching.

The gliding hawk called above them, a high, piercing wail carried by the wind, and Shelley felt suddenly as though its cry rent a tear in the thick casing around her heart. Emotion welled up inside her, and it wasn't fear or sorrow or rage. It felt safe and solid, and it made her smile. It felt so…good. Just good. Completely good.

And she knew that it wasn't the hawk that had brought her this; it had been Blue's words.

Her lip trembled. Her eyes filled with tears.

Then more emotion. Humility. She didn't deserve his commitment, his affection, but he gave it anyway, freely, generously. She might never be able to give him any more than she had already, and he knew it. Still, he gave, and his gifts were in his eyes, true and fair.

When she could bear no more, she closed her eyes. One tear slid down each cheek, and Blue wiped them away with his thumb.

When she opened her eyes, a tremulous smile burst forth unbidden.

"Thank you," she whispered.

He caught her head in the crook of his elbow and dropped a kiss on top of her head. "Let's go."

They changed in the rest rooms by the trailhead, then headed up the path. When Blue found the place where he wanted to pray, Shelley sat quietly nearby on a lichen-covered rock, closing her eyes to give him more privacy. The mountain smelled wonderful, of earth and rock, of pine, sage, juniper and grass. A bird landed close to her with much ruffling of wings and branches, and she opened her eyes. A jay. She saw that Blue had placed a garland of small red bundles tied together with string in a pine bough. They were tobacco offerings he had said, prayer ties, each one representing a prayer. Some, she knew, were for her. It was a comforting thought.

When he was finished, they went back down the mountain, down the road, back to the highways and at last into the Black Hills.

Later, when the desk clerk at the Bullock Hotel confirmed their reservations for two rooms, Shelley caught Blue's arm.

"One room will be fine," she said.

He looked at her carefully. "You're sure?"

She held his gaze. "I'm sure."

His smile had promises in it.

Chapter Ten

Shelley was on her way upstairs while Blue emptied his pocket change into a slot machine before it struck her: it was her wedding night, and she didn't have anything to wear that was remotely sexy. She hadn't been ready to sleep with Blue when she'd packed this morning, and all she had with her was the white flannel nightgown her mother had given her in anticipation of a cold South Dakota winter. Come to think of it, between the flannel and a near twin in cooler cotton, she didn't own a single piece of sexy lingerie.

She knew Blue wouldn't mind, but it bothered her. He had been treating their marriage with respect and care, honoring the bond they had forged even if it wasn't the kind of marriage he would have ideally wanted. He had honored her, first with the ring last night, then this afternoon at Bear Butte with his simple, gracious words. She wanted to give him something back, something to please him, even something as insignificant as pretty frills on his wedding night.

Maybe she would ask Blue if they couldn't stop at the mall Sunday before driving back to Gilbert. For tonight, though, the flannel would have to suffice.

Oh, dear, she couldn't believe she was obsessing about a nightgown when she didn't know if she'd made the right decision about making love with Blue.

Concentrate on him, not me. Give him this, she told herself.

She had showered and swathed herself in the granny gown when a soft knock sounded at the door. Her heart trip-hammered as she turned to face the door.

When he came in, his chuckle surprised her. "Careful. If your eyes get any bigger, I'm going to feel like a marauding savage about to have his wicked way with some frightened Victorian schoolmarm."

She had the grace to laugh. "You startled me. And I am a schoolmarm. Sort of. The contemporary equivalent, I guess."

He closed the door behind him and secured the locks. "That nightgown looks like it came straight out of the nineteenth century." Slowly, he approached, looking her up and down. "Your body is completely hidden in that thing."

The way his eyes lingered on her breasts made her doubt that he was being entirely honest. "It was a gift from my mother," she said. *Look at him,* she reminded herself. *Don't think. Look at how his hair looks so dark and sleek in the lamplight. Look at the way his shoulders fill out his shirt so beautifully.* "It's for South Dakota winters."

"Figures. Mothers never think their beautiful daughters might prefer South Dakota men to keep them warm."

He tossed his keys and wallet onto the dresser, his eyes never leaving her. "You're naked under that thing, aren't you?"

Look at how snug his jeans fit his thighs. Remember what he looks like when he comes in from riding in the morning...all hot and so perfectly male?

She took a step toward him.

He snagged a handful of her gown and brought her the rest of the way. When she was flush against him, he slipped his hands under her arms and ran them slowly down her sides from her armpits to the tops of her thighs. His thumbs contoured her breasts, catching on her nipples.

They were hard before he touched her.

His fingers scraped over her back, then her hips, digging in to mold her flesh under his hands. She leaned into him.

"Oh, yes." His heart beat harder under her breast. "You are most definitely naked under this."

Crushing her closer, he buried his face in the curve of her neck and inhaled deeply. "I love how you smell." He kissed her neck, licked, then bit her lightly, only to lave the spot with his tongue once more.

Sparkling sensations rocketed down the sensitive muscles in her neck and sent her up on tiptoe, pressing closer.

He growled in satisfaction and repeated his attentions. By the time he lifted his head to gaze down at her, her stomach felt like she'd plummeted a thousand feet sixteen times over. Her back tingled, her breasts itched and she ached for him.

"You make me so hot," he breathed.

She pulled his head down to kiss him, to keep the sensations flowing. She wanted to taste him again, to roll her hands over the firm muscles of his arms and back.

Her first kiss was chaste, a greeting. With the second, she licked his lip the way he had done to her before. The third time, she took his full lower lip between her own and sucked. When she opened her mouth fully to him, he surged into the kiss, taking it from her, then giving it back. Desire built to a higher pitch, and she let it mount.

The decision had been made.

Don't think.

Touch.

Kiss.

Enjoy.

Blue pulled back. "I should take a shower."

"No." She buried her nose in the open placket of his shirt and breathed him in, warm, musky, with a faint trace of the soap he used.

"You're sure?" He raised her chin to look at him.

He was giving her the chance to back out. For a fleeting moment, a voice inside clamored for reprieve.

Don't think. She used the words like a mantra.

Touch.

She touched his collarbone, let her fingers glide beneath his shirt, trace the bone, find the hollows. He was so smooth, so strong.

Kiss.

She kissed his chin, flicked her tongue along his jaw. It was almost smooth, with only a few whiskers to tease her mouth. She kissed his mouth again, delving in to taste him.

"I'm sure."

"Then hang on." He swept her off her feet, and carried her to the big, old-fashioned bed, laying her down carefully. He slung his shirt over his head before he lay down with her.

His weight felt good beside her on the bed. He lifted

one hand and caressed her cheek, running his thumb over her mouth. With studied concentration, he explored her with his hand through the heavy flannel. Strong brown fingers lingered at her neck, causing her to gasp as she had when he'd kissed her there. They stroked every inch of her chest, then descended to cup her breasts, one at a time, testing their weight beneath the nightgown, pushing, gently squeezing, his thumb rubbing over each nipple until she arched her back, groaning with the need he nurtured.

His hand moved lower, to her belly, and he dipped his head to take one nipple into his mouth, pulling with his teeth, teasing her with his tongue. The pleasure made her gasp, which thrust her breast up for him, an obvious plea for more. All the while, his hand laid claim to the slightly rounded curve of her belly, tracing from hipbone to hipbone, fingers catching in her navel, ranging higher, brushing the underside of the breast he wasn't suckling, then down again, each time inching lower.

Excitement made her arch and writhe under his touch. She began to feel impatient for his hands on her bare skin. Automatically, she bunched the white flannel up in her fist, drawing it up her legs.

Blue caught her movement and found the hem of the nightie, pushing it higher, dragging his hand over the naked skin of her calf, then her thigh. When he reached the top of her leg, he slid his hand around to cup her bottom and released her breast.

Passion made his eyes darker than night. He took her gown in both hands. "Ready?"

She nodded and raised her arms and her hips. He whisked the white flannel over her head before tossing it to the floor.

"Shelley, you're beautiful." He touched her breast

lightly, as if it were made of gossamer, then bent to parade kisses down the middle of her, starting at her lips. In measured time, he kissed her mouth, the hollow at the base of her throat, her heart between her breasts, each nipple, her solar plexus, her navel, the center of her belly, the soft brown hair a little lower. Then he licked and nibbled his way back to her mouth. "So beautiful," he breathed. "Perfect mouth, perfect throat, perfect breasts. All of you. Every inch is perfect. You're so soft, so sweet."

Wonder and humility washed over her again, but this time they were tempered by arousal. Blue was a generous lover, and his desire fed her own. She coaxed his tongue into her mouth, circled it with her own, tasted his passion.

Touch. Touch him. Be generous with him.

She reached for him, found his belt, pulled it free. Where her fingers brushed his stomach, his skin was hot. She tugged impatiently, and he ended their kiss to help her with his belt. Then it only took a moment for him to kick off his shoes and shove his jeans and briefs to the floor.

Touch again. Share his passion.

She reached for him, wanting him so badly her hands shook. He was smooth as silk, rising strong and straight from a small nest of dark curls. With her other hand, she found the hard curve of his backside, also hot, so firm. He was all heat and hard flesh, smooth, strong, wonderfully male.

"You're beautiful," she whispered, urging him closer. "I like touching you."

He groaned, taking himself out of her hands. "I love having your hands on me." He levered over her, supporting most of his weight on his arms.

Their legs tangled, and she sighed. One of his thighs

pushed between hers and she let his weight make a place for him there. He snuggled his thigh against her and bent to kiss her mouth again.

"How fast do you want to take this?" he said into her mouth. A quick nip followed.

She arched and he surged against her thigh. She nipped him back, then felt another surge. "Now. I'm ready."

She spread her hands over his back, kneading his flesh, running her palms over pliant muscle and solid bone. How could he be so hot? Every inch of him radiated warmth like a stoked furnace. Everywhere he touched her she felt so deliciously warm. She squirmed under him, fitting herself more fully to his heat, reveling in his body.

He skimmed a hand down her side, toying briefly with her breast, then moving confidently to nudge her legs farther apart. Gladly, she opened to him, eager for his touch, all reservations forgotten in the need for his touch.

She captured his head and pulled his mouth to hers, fully open, questing for the taste of him. Exploring his mouth again, she opened her legs more fully, invited him to touch her more intimately yet.

Warm fingers rubbed her lightly. It felt strange, almost foreign to be touched this way after so long. At the same time, it felt glorious, and she wanted more.

Suckling his tongue, she pushed rational thought away, and lifted her hips just a bit to give him better access.

One finger found her most sensitive skin and stroked down over it, sending a convulsion through her. Again. Another jolt. Then he stroked all the way down, his finger sinking into soft, wet heat.

"More," she gasped. "Please."

He released a hissing, pent-up breath, then a low groan. He took over the kiss again, thrusting his tongue against hers, suckling her mouth. He took over her body, slipping a finger inside her, while still rubbing her with his thumb.

Desire overtook everything. Shelley gave herself over to it, gave herself to Blue. Each stroke of his thumb, each press of his hand spun her closer to release.

"I want you inside me. Please, Blue. Now." She didn't recognize the low, throbbing voice as her own. She only knew that she wanted him more than she had ever wanted anyone.

This time he didn't hesitate or ask if she was sure. He moved her legs wider apart with his knee, and brought her hand to him.

He was even harder than he had been. She held him while he readied the condom, then slipped it on.

Then he slipped inside her. Sharp pleasure brought her off the bed, made her grab his shoulders, and rock into his thrust. He was so much more than a friend. He was her lover, now, her husband, and she instinctively strove to match his heat and passion.

He held her still beneath him for a moment, his arms straining, his head thrown back. Then he bent again to kiss her. Out he slid. Another kiss. Then in. He caught her nipple with his lips and sucked hard. Out. Then in again slowly.

She found his buttocks and together they found a rhythm that carried them both toward completion.

In those final moments, the crack that had started in her armor around her heart opened wider. First came a welling of passionate satisfaction, an exultation of both body and heart. Then came the wonder and the humility, the abiding sense that she was blessed by Blue's care.

"You're incredible," she whispered, cradling his head on her breast. "You make me feel things..." She broke off, unable to articulate her emotions. "It's been so long."

Then from the core of her, a deep, wrenching sorrow welled, unbidden and unwelcome. It had been so long. She had lost too much to deny, and as her heart opened to Blue, it also opened to her grief.

It started with small tremors that she couldn't control. Hot tears leaked from her eyes, and her belly heaved as she tried to stop the sobs she knew were coming.

Blue slipped out of her and tried to gather her in his arms. "It's okay."

She rolled away from him, ashamed of herself, but unable to stop. The sorrow lanced deep, a physical pain that felt as though she had been sundered through to her backbone and left open to bleed her heart dry. She should have died from this pain. Instead, it grew sharper, intensified by the regret she felt for being unable to hold it in.

Tonight of all nights, she didn't want this grief. She had wanted to give this night to Blue as a gift, and now all she could do was sob her heart out for what she had lost so many years ago.

Blue curled his body around her, patting her back, sharing his warmth when she felt like ice. Except for the tears. They were so hot.

"I'm s-sorry," she said, barely able to form the words through the tears.

"It's okay."

"I don't w-want you to...to see...I wanted t-tonight to be special." Her words were distorted, racked with sobs.

"It was perfect. You're perfect. You just need to cry now. There's nothing wrong with that." He rocked her in his arms. "My uncle, the holy man, always told us when we were kids that crying is a kind of prayer. It lets God know you really need his help.''

That made her sob harder.

Dear God, she thought, I do need help. I need so much help. I need courage most of all. The courage to go on. The courage to let go.

It had never seemed further from her.

She cried, and Blue held her until she fell into an exhausted sleep.

After a night of fitful sleep, Blue awakened in the gray dawn. Shelley lay beside him, once again wrapped in the flannel nightgown she'd retrieved and put on when she woke briefly around midnight. She lay on her side, facing him, one hand tucked under her cheek, and he wanted her again. Last night had only served to increase his desire. The lovemaking had been fantastic, incredible really, for a first time.

Then she had trusted him enough to let him see her tears and to hold her while she cried. She hadn't wanted to, he knew, but she'd allowed her feelings to show. If he knew anything about Shelley, it was that she had kept her feelings to herself for a very long time. If she let him see her grief, he hoped it was because somewhere in her heart, she felt safe enough with him that she was beginning to let go.

The thought roused quiet pride in him and a deepened desire to protect her, to make everything better. Maybe that wasn't entirely healthy, knowing as he did that Shelley had to make things better herself. But he loved thinking he might make a difference in her life, that their marriage wasn't just for him, so he could get joint custody of Libby and Travis sooner.

He brushed her hair back from her face, a feather touch

that didn't cause her to so much as stir. The tiny frown she wore so often was absent; instead, her face was relaxed in sleep, lips curved as if she was lost in happy dreams.

He'd been more surprised yesterday that she had decided to sleep with him than he had been by the tears that followed their lovemaking. He hoped her dreams were good.

Watching her, he thought about waking her with lovemaking. After last night, he was pretty sure she would be wary of any further sexual intimacy, afraid of the feelings it would rouse. He didn't think the next time would be as hard for her, but he also wasn't sure she'd realize that. He was tempted to try to engage her natural passion before she was awake enough to stop him.

That would be manipulative, he knew full well. He shouldn't do it. He should talk to her about what had happened, let her discover on her own that she didn't need to fear her emotions so much. If she had anger and grief to work through, he understood.

But he was getting to know Shelley pretty well, and he doubted that she would discover this in any sort of timely fashion. It could take her months to be willing to make love with him again. He didn't want to wait months. He didn't want to wait another fifteen minutes.

In the end, rock-hard desire and hands that itched to touch her made the decision for him. He reached for her, and she responded with sleepy pleasure to his hands roaming her body in increasingly intimate ways. As her body strained with his, her hands held fast to his shoulders.

There were no tears this time. But the smile she gave him when it was over never reached her eyes, and Blue worried that instead of learning to trust the passion between them, she was learning to wall herself off from him even when she made love.

It was a thought that made him sick inside.

Chapter Eleven

By the middle of October, the leaves on the elms surrounding the house had turned golden and begun to fall. Sumac glowed in shades of garnet and violet in the ditches along the highways, and high up in the cool, blue sky, geese fled south in wide V's. Pheasant season came, and Shelley took to wearing a hunter's orange vest when she walked the fields.

Life had settled into patterns that were partly familiar, partly new to her. The accustomed progress of the school year helped Shelley adjust to the new parts of her life, such as being married again.

One aspect of being married to Blue was regular visits from Marilyn Tall Feather until he had a decision on his joint-custody petition. Rounding the bend west of the house after an afternoon walk, Shelley saw Marilyn's big Buick approach on the section road, then slow down and turn into their drive.

Blue wasn't back yet from cross-country practice. That meant Marilyn wanted to talk to her alone, and Shelley wondered why.

She reached the gate as Marilyn was getting out of her car.

"Good afternoon, Shelley." As she always did, Marilyn gave the impression of painstaking professionalism. As late as it was in the afternoon, her simply cut burgundy suit, cream-colored shell and matching pumps looked as fresh as they probably had early that morning. "You're looking comfortable this afternoon."

Shelley felt rumpled and dirty in her worn jeans, plaid flannel shirt and Blue's neon orange hunting west. "Hello, Marilyn. Blue isn't back from practice yet."

"Yes, I know. I was just over at the high school. I saw him at the track with the team. I was hoping to talk to you alone today."

That's what Shelley had been afraid of. "Please come in." She held the gate and followed Marilyn.

Once they were seated on the old sofa with cups of tea, Marilyn got straight to business.

"How did things go when you met Libby and Travis last week?"

She and Blue had driven to Casper the previous weekend. Shelley hadn't wanted to go, thinking it was too soon, but Marilyn had been pressing Blue about it.

"It went quite well. I was surprised." Shelley sipped her tea. "The phone conversations we'd been having helped. That was a good idea." Marilyn was full of helpful ideas. She was doing everything she could to assist Blue, and Shelley didn't know why she just wished Marilyn would leave them alone.

"What did you think of the children?"

Shelley took her time answering, knowing how much

Blue had at stake. "They're bright. Interested in a lot of things, both socially and intellectually. Travis is an affectionate, good-natured little boy."

"What about Libby?" Marilyn prompted.

"We got along well. She seemed to accept me, which says a lot for her. Not all thirteen-year-old girls would be accepting of a stepmother who appears out of nowhere."

"What did you think of her as a person?"

Shelley tapped a nail on her cup. She didn't want to say anything that might make it harder for Blue to get the kids, and she didn't want to sound so positive that Marilyn wouldn't take her answer seriously. She decided to be honest, if cautious. "She made a few offhand comments that worried me. Something about Indian girls being naturally wild, and several cynical remarks that surprised me. Also I think she has an older boyfriend. I'm not sure how much older, but that's not usually a good sign."

"No." Marilyn waited for her to continue.

"I think she may be depressed." She stared at the rim of her cup. "I think she's holding in a lot of feelings, not expressing them directly."

Marilyn's gaze never wavered. "That's something you understand well, isn't it?"

Here it was, the underlying reason for this visit. Shelley wondered if Blue had said something to Marilyn. "I think most people understand being depressed."

"Depression can be a natural response in a variety of situations. It allows people to heal, gather strength to face changes. As long as they don't get caught up in retreat or bitterness, most people who suffer from bouts of depression don't experience any lasting ill effects."

They were no longer talking about Libby, and both of them knew it.

Marilyn's expression was bland, a classic therapist's pose. Shelley had seen it often enough to recognize it in an instant. "How are you adjusting to married life?"

Shelley forced herself to smile. "Very well, thank you."

"It must have been a big change for you."

"Yes, but it's a welcome change." Her statement wasn't exactly a lie. Marrying Blue had changed her life more than she had thought it would, and she had wanted change. It was still difficult, though. From the first day of their marriage, he had treated her as a real wife, a partner, giving her his full commitment and loyalty. He treated her with love, even if he wasn't in love with her, and he seemed naturally to expect the same from her.

That unspoken expectation was not always easy to meet, even if it was good for her. It kept her from protesting when he suggested that they share her room and turn his into a study for both of them until they converted it into a bedroom for Travis. It had prodded her to talk to Libby and Travis on the phone, then to go with him to Wyoming to meet them. It kept her in bed with him at night when she wanted to escape into the old fog.

She knew the changes her marriage required were healthy, despite the struggles they presented. Part of her wanted those changes and the promises they held. With Blue, there were moments when she was able to conceive of a future marked by happiness and love, a future for the two of them together with his children as a family. It was a powerful lure, one that sometimes reached through all the layers of her resistance.

"I needed a change," she reiterated for Marilyn.

"It hasn't been too much too fast?"

It was an ironic question from the woman who had precipitated the marriage with her adamant insistence on stability and upholding social standards.

"It's been a lot of change. So far, I'm doing okay."

"Blue seems very happy."

Shelley looked into her cup of cooling tea with a small smile.

"If I can be honest, Shelley, you don't seem as happy as he does. I'm a little concerned about you."

"You needn't be. I'm doing very well. Blue is a wonderful man, and everything is fine."

Marilyn's silence felt like a condemnation.

"I'm glad," she said at last. "Oh, I thought you'd like to know that Rachel Tom is working with Vivian Garreaux, Bethany's mother, again. She's trying to find her a rehab placement."

"Thank you for letting me know." Shelley had filed her report of suspected physical abuse a month ago when Bethany had come to school with a badly cut lip, a gash at her hairline and scratches on her hands.

"How is Bethany doing in your class?"

"Not as well as she should. She's missed at least one day every week since the beginning of school, and she's only turned in one assignment. She's not passing."

Marilyn sighed, showing more compassion than Shelley expected. "The only classes she's passing are health and PE. I'm afraid she's going to drop out as soon as she turns sixteen."

"That would be a shame."

"It certainly would." Marilyn set her teacup on the packing-crate table. "Shelley, if I could convince Bethany to work harder on her schoolwork, would you be willing to tutor her after school once or twice a week?"

"Of course I would, but Bethany doesn't like me very much. I'm not sure she'd agree to work with me."

"She's just a little jealous of you. Like a lot of teenagers, she's had a crush on an older man." She gave Shelley a conspiratorial look. "Your husband."

It still sounded strange to hear Blue referred to as her husband. "Yes, I'd noticed."

"Let her get to know you better. She'll get over it quickly."

Bethany Garreaux was not easy for Shelley to be around. The girl seemed to focus a tremendous amount of Shelley's rage. The day Bethany had come in so battered, Shelley hadn't been sure she would get through the period without breaking down. Through sheer dint of will, she had, but she'd spent her prep period in the teacher's rest room crying, so furious with Bethany's mother she would have gladly given the woman some of her own medicine. The strength of her reaction, and her inability to control it, frightened her.

But she couldn't say no to helping Bethany. "If Bethany's willing, I'd be glad to try. I'll talk to Steve to set it up."

"That's wonderful. I need to get back to the office now." Marilyn collected her purse and rose.

Outside, she took Shelley's hand and patted it as a mother might. The gesture surprised Shelley.

"If you ever need someone to talk to, Shelley, I hope you'll feel you can come to me. About Bethany, or anything else."

"Thank you, Marilyn." The older woman released her hand. "I'll remember that."

Shelley couldn't imagine talking to Marilyn about the things that bothered her, about the way she wished she could pull back from Blue sometimes, from her students, especially students like Bethany, for whom life was so complicated, and from her own feelings. Since that awful night when she'd sobbed for over an hour in Blue's arms, she'd been so wary, trying to control her feelings, but she couldn't always. Sometimes it was too hard to keep everything on an even keel.

Blue made it hard. Her job made it hard. At times the rage and the grief seemed so close to the surface, so ready to burst forth and disrupt the control that carried her through each day and each night. Sometimes, like that day at school with Bethany, she couldn't keep her emotions in check.

Even letting in the good things she felt with Blue was dangerous. The affection they shared was wonderful, their friendship solid and supportive, but when she truly let him touch her feelings, his warmth triggered more than an answering affection in her. On occasion, it sent her into despondency because she wasn't able to give him as much as he gave her. At other times, it made her angry with him, because it seemed so easy for him to transcend the harsh feelings she couldn't escape. She didn't want to be angry with him, not for any reason. Her anger frightened her.

Similarly, the passion they shared was exciting, a source of mutual pleasure, but with it came a lowering of defenses that made it difficult to hold at bay the negative emotions she didn't want to own. Worst of all, if she dared to hope that someday they might have a real marriage based on a love they both openly embraced, she thought about what it would feel like to lose him. Yes, sometimes the good things about Blue made keeping her anger and grief bottled up harder, so she stayed on the surface, even when they made love. She stayed in her body, tucking her spirit way down deep inside her, hidden even from her own heart.

She didn't know what else to do.

Neither did she know how long she could go on this way.

Bethany wasn't in class the next day, but after school, Shelley found her at the track, dressed for practice.

Blue was there, too, looking the quintessential coach in his sweats and baseball cap, whistle and stopwatch dangling on cords around his neck, clipboard in hand.

He walked over to greet her, wearing a pleased expression. "Howdy, pardner," he drawled. "Come to run with us this afternoon?" He dropped a quick kiss on her cheek to scattered applause from the students watching.

"No running for me. I'll stick to learning to ride better for now." Blue had brought his horses, Jewel and Crunch, to their place a month ago. Shelley had ridden Jewel, a pretty bay mare, a few times. Crunch, a much bigger palomino gelding, aptly named by Travis for his tendency to chomp on anything in reach, had gained her respect if not her affection. "Maybe I should start practicing so I can get out of Crunch's way faster."

"He'll love you when he gets to know you better. You don't need to be so scared of him. He was standoffish with the kids at first, too, but now he loves them."

"He tried to eat my shoe," she reminded him. "With my foot still in it."

"He's just a baby. He'll grow out of that." He grinned at her. "What brings you out here?"

"Bethany wasn't in class today. I wanted to talk to her about her grades."

"She's got three more weeks until the quarter's over.

If she doesn't have a *C* average, she's off the team.'' He was adamant.

"Can you spare her for ten minutes?"

"Sure." He blew the whistle. "Garreaux!" When Bethany looked up from a stretch, he motioned her over.

Rising, she ambled toward them, exchanging quips and laughing with the other cross-country runners on her way.

"She doesn't do anything on anyone else's time, does she?" Blue chuckled. "If she were my kid, we'd have a little talk about that."

"If she were your kid, she wouldn't have so much to prove."

"Libby seems to have plenty to prove."

"Not like Bethany does." She tucked her hands into the pockets of her linen jacket.

"Thank God for that," he said softly.

Bethany approached, arms swinging in an exaggerated arc. "Hey, it's the March County High newlyweds. What can I do for you, Mr. and Mrs. Larson?"

"Ms. Mathews," Blue corrected. Shelley had preferred to keep her own name.

"No point in changing your name when you're not planning on sticking around, is there?" Bethany tossed her head and set one hand on her hip. She reminded Shelley of Crunch just before he planned to take a bite out of something—or someone.

Blue didn't take her any more seriously than he took Crunch. He ruffled her hair and bumped her off balance. "That's just wishful thinking on your part, kiddo. Shelley isn't going anywhere, so you might as well be nice. She likes you."

Shelley watched Bethany's expression morph through aggravation at being called "kiddo" to surprised interest when Blue said she liked her.

"This isn't about my missing class today?" Bethany asked.

"Only indirectly," Shelley replied.

"Ten minutes, Ms. Mathews. Then this girl's going to run her heart out for me." He leaned toward Shelley and surprised her with a kiss on the mouth. He'd jogged off before Shelley could react.

Bethany rolled her eyes. "I suppose he's so in love with you he can't help himself," she intoned with the unparalleled sarcasm of a jealous fifteen-year-old. "It's disgusting."

Her words froze Shelley's heart for a long moment. Blue in love with her? He wasn't, but she couldn't very well deny that to Bethany. Normally confident in her abilities to talk to students, even about difficult matters, Shelley felt as if she were sinking in quicksand with Bethany.

Maybe she should just lighten up.

"He's a pretty good kisser. I wouldn't want him to stop." It popped out. Shelley was almost as surprised as Bethany, but she quickly took advantage of the moment to bring up the matter of grades. "Hey, we need to talk about your grade in my class. You've got a *D*-minus right now. If you want to run, we've got to do something about that."

Bethany sighed melodramatically. "More reasons why it stinks having your coach married to your history teacher."

"Do you want to run?" Shelley made the question as low-key as she could, no challenge, no rhetorical spin, only a real question.

Bethany stared at her feet. "Yeah. I love to run. It's the best thing I've got. Sometimes I think maybe it's the only thing I've got." Her voice was uncharacteristically quiet.

Shelley felt tears start in her eyes. Why did this girl touch her emotions so easily? She blinked the tears back.

"Blue says you have more talent than anyone he's ever seen in high-school long-distance events. I say you have more brains than you probably know what to do with. Bethany, you can get an *A* in my class and every other class on your schedule if you want to."

Bethany's almond-shaped eyes were huge when she lifted them to look at Shelley. "You don't understand." It was a flat, factual statement.

The wind clattered into a tiny dust devil, chasing a few dried leaves between them.

"Maybe not."

"I can't always come to school."

"Because of your mother."

Bethany didn't say anything.

"You know, sometimes we have to deal with situations that are beyond our control. It's easy to let them control us."

"What do you know about it?" Bethany sneered. "Don't preach at me. You've had everything go your way all your life."

"No, I haven't," Shelley said, her voice fierce with anger. "My first husband was killed in a drive-by shooting four years ago. I have *not* had everything my way all my life. What's more, I haven't handled it very well. I've wasted years trying to figure out how to go on. Years! I let the situation control me. I can't change what happened. I hate it. It was wrong. Just like your mother being an alcoholic is wrong. But you don't have to let her ruin your life."

Shelley was shaking so hard she thought she might sink to her knees on the grass.

Bethany stared at her. "I'm sorry. I didn't know."

"Thank you." She took a deep breath. "I know you didn't. It's not something I find easy to talk about."

"Sometimes talking helps." Bethany scowled at the ground. "Maybe…"

"What?"

"Nothing." She turned to look at the bare hills rising to the south, and Shelley knew Bethany wasn't going to finish whatever it was she had been about to say.

She tucked her hands into her coat pockets, willing her hands to steady, her voice to relax. "Bethany, don't give up what you love the most. If you love to run, then let's find a way to make you free to run. I'll help."

"Why?"

"I'm not sure."

"You don't have to."

"I want to."

"I don't need help," Bethany insisted.

"No, maybe you don't," Shelley agreed. "You're bright and you're resourceful. You could bring your grades up on your own."

"That's right. I could."

"Maybe *I* need help."

Bethany's eyes flashed back to Shelley's face. "With what? With talking about what happened?"

"Maybe that's part of it. I'm not sure I can explain it."

Bethany stared at her, the suspicion in her dark eyes gradually giving way to simple speculation.

"I never had a teacher talk to me like this before," Bethany finally said.

"Probably not." Her hands had stopped shaking. "I'll tell you what. If you'd like to work with me for an hour after school on Tuesdays and Thursdays, I'll work out a schedule with Blue so you don't miss practice time. We'll work on history, and I can help you with math and biology, as well. What do you say?"

Blue's whistle sounded. "Garreaux!" he yelled. "One minute!"

Bethany glanced back at him, then bit her lip. "Can we try it for a week? See how it works? Then I'll let you know."

"Sure. Next Tuesday, then. Right after last period."

"I gotta go." She loped off.

Shelley watched her run, wondering what it was she needed from this girl, knowing there was something, not at all sure what it was. As far as she could tell, Bethany Garreaux was only going to make her cry again.

Chapter Twelve

That evening, Shelley came home late from her Lakota history class at the college. Blue met her at the door.

"Put your books down and let's go out for a few minutes. There's something I want to show you."

Outside, he led her along the track that wound northwest of the house, away from the bright security light, out of sight of the lights from town. They walked in companionable silence.

"Did you know the Lakota had their own constellations in the old days?"

"No. Did you learn them as a child?"

He shook his head. "If my mom knew them, she never said. I should ask her. Some of the people at the tribal college over on the Rosebud have done some research, put out a book. They learned about old star maps made on hides, so old no one remembers when they were made. As old as the Sacred Pipe."

"We learned about the Buffalo Calf Pipe in my class." It was an ancient, sacred pipe, given to the Lakota people by the Buffalo Calf Woman so long ago it was hard to tell how old it really was.

"Look up at the Big Dipper." He stood behind Shelley and pointed over her shoulder. "There used to be another star in the middle of the dipper. It's supposed to be a black hole now, I think. But in the old days, that's where Falling Star fell through the sky to come to earth. He was a great hero."

"Like Hercules?"

"Same type."

"What did Falling Star do?"

"Lots of things. He saved the seven sisters that are the seven points on Harney Peak in the Black Hills. He put them in the sky as the Seven Sisters. He saved people from hunger when the buffalo went away. He sacrificed himself all the time for the people."

Shelley was learning that giving of oneself was a much valued Lakota virtue. "A true hero, then."

"Mmm. Like what you did today for Bethany."

Shelley closed her eyes and leaned back into him. The air seemed colder suddenly, and she sought his warmth. She didn't want to think of working with Bethany as anything special. It was nothing she wouldn't do for any of her students who needed the extra help. It was her job. "What did she say?"

"That you're going to tutor her."

Shelley opened her eyes to stare at the heavens again. The stars shone fiercely in a moonless sky. "Anything else?"

"She asked me to tell you she won't tell anyone what you told her." He brushed her hair back and tucked it behind her ear. "You told her about your first husband, didn't you?"

Her first husband. How odd that sounded. And now she had another. "Yes." The word slipped out as a breath, the merest whisper.

"That took courage, *cantesicela*. It was a sacrifice." He kissed her temple. "I think it helped."

"It just happened. I didn't mean to do it." She wished she hadn't.

"Do you have to mean to do something to make it brave? My brothers used to talk about that when they got back from Vietnam." Shelley knew his oldest brothers were ten and twelve years older than he was, old enough to have gone to Vietnam as young men. "There are lots of types of courage. I don't think all of them require thinking about it first."

"Maybe not."

"I know things are hard for you, Shelley." Another kiss. "I know I make it hard sometimes."

"No…"

"Yes," he contradicted. "I see when you want to hide, to go back into yourself. Especially when we make love."

There was no use denying it. He was too perceptive. "I wish I could give you more."

"You don't have to hide from me. I won't hurt you."

"It's not you I'm afraid of, I don't think."

They watched the stars together in silence for a while. She couldn't explain to him why, but she did still need to retreat from all the change, all the emotion that threatened to overwhelm her.

"That center place in the bowl of the dipper," he said, picking up the thread of their earlier conversation, "that's where souls are supposed to go in and out of the spirit world. When we die and our spirit moves on, we go through where that old star was. It's a gateway. An opening."

She looked up, imagining making the long climb high up into the sky and finding a gateway to a new world. In the world she imagined, there were no battered teenage girls, no gang challenges that sent children into the streets with deadly weapons, no aching years of pain and grief for anyone. She imagined a world where she could love again. "I like that idea."

"In the old days, people went back and forth all the time."

"Not now."

"That makes you sad."

Wind stirred in the cedars nearby.

He turned her in his arms and kissed her, one of his impossibly sweet, gentle kisses. His lips were cold, but they warmed quickly.

"I want to make love to you, *mitawin.*" *Wife,* he called her now, when he wanted to make love, not *sad heart.*

Tucking herself more fully into his arms, she murmured her assent. She never denied him her body. Making love with Blue was pleasurable, and her body responded to his more and more easily as he learned what pleased her best.

But her heart was still too often sad, and it lay between them like a stone, fixed and unyielding, blocking the love Shelley knew might have grown between them had she met him in a different life. For a moment, she wished she could fly up into the sky and pass through the center of the dipper's bowl into another life, a life where she could come to Blue whole and able to give freely from her heart. She wished she might have met him before everything had changed.

The thought startled her. Before Brad's death? Before she had lost him, she had been married. She couldn't have loved Blue then. She wouldn't have. Before she met Brad? *Instead* of Brad?

Guilt rocked through her, and she turned Blue so that she could look over his shoulder at the dipper while he placed slow, lingering kisses down her neck.

If she could go back and forth to the spirit world, if she could have Brad back, visit him, would she want to?

Up until this moment, she would have answered with a resounding yes. Wouldn't she? Now she understood that answer meant not having Blue in her life. As his mother had said, she couldn't have two husbands.

All sorts of disturbing thoughts filled her mind. The life she had now was so different from what she'd had before, she hadn't really made conscious comparisons between Brad and Blue.

She wondered if that was because she hadn't let herself.

It wasn't fair to compare them at all. Brad had been so much younger, so focused on his career. Blue was older, so of course he was more mature and wiser. If he was more generous with himself than Brad had been, it was because he had learned to be. Brad had never had the time. Med students had notoriously demanding schedules.

If Blue had learned in a few short months to touch her body in ways that made her cry out in mindless pleasure, even while her heart still mourned, it wasn't that he was a better lover than Brad had been. Brad would have learned.

Her traitorous mind reminded her that Brad hadn't learned so much in more than seven years with her. But he would have, she insisted to herself.

"What's wrong?" Blue stopped kissing her to peer at her, his brows knit in concern.

"I was just thinking."

"Want to tell me?"

She gave a tiny shake of her head and stared at the bowl of the dipper.

Blue noted the direction of her gaze and sighed. "Do you want to follow him?"

Shelley didn't answer immediately, her eyes lingering on the sky. When she looked back at Blue, she saw more than concern in the taut line of his mouth. He was angry, as well.

He wasn't such a paragon, after all.

"Shelley, do you want to follow him?" he repeated. There was more than concern, more than anger in his voice this time. Was it jealousy she heard? Or was it fear?

"Not tonight." And she realized as she said it that she didn't. Out of nowhere, a chuckle escaped her, and Blue looked more puzzled than ever. "Come on," she said, looping her arm through his and turning them both back toward the house. "My husband just told me he wanted to make love with me. I don't want to keep him waiting."

Blue lagged a fraction of a step behind her, then swept her into a brisk pace.

Later, when she lay naked and wanting at his side, Shelley tried to hold her heart open to Blue. She left the light on, and she let herself see the pleasure in his face. If she didn't know better, she might have called it love. Whatever it was, it touched her, and she let the pleasure and the humility and the wonder into her heart without thinking about the tears that might come later.

It wasn't until morning, when she awoke wrapped in Blue's arms, that she realized the tears had never come.

* * *

By the beginning of November, a series of hard freezes had come and gone, dressing the prairie landscape in a winter palette of buff and brown and the pale blue of the sky, fading now as the sun traveled south and the land grew colder. Having completed a successful tutoring session with Bethany, Shelley eyed the high clouds from the window of her classroom, wondering when they would thicken and bring the season's first snow. Blue said it would be soon.

With the heedless excitement peculiar to small children and those raised in sunny climes, Shelley hoped when it did snow that it would come as a regular blizzard. Already she'd stocked the house well with staples and emergency supplies. Blue had laughed at her when he'd seen the mountain of toilet paper stacked on shelves in the basement, but she didn't care. She wanted to see drifts of snow up to the car-shed eaves. She wanted to be tucked away all snug and tight in her little house with Blue and Shoonk. Together, they would be safe, secure and warm.

Packing up her books and the assignments she needed to grade that evening, Shelley grinned to herself. The real appeal of a blizzard, she knew, was spending a whole day and a night with Blue. There would be no classes, no students, no cross-country practice, nothing but hours to wile away.

Shelley had a pretty good idea how Blue would want to spend most of those hours. And the way things had been going, she wasn't averse to the prospect of a day or two alone with him at all.

The past two weeks had gone astonishingly well, both at work and at home. The tutoring sessions with Bethany had had a few bumps the first day or two, but shortly settled into a productive pattern. Shelley had already seen a marked improvement in Bethany's class work, and she hadn't missed a day in two weeks—a record.

Aside from Bethany, her classes were going well. The students were responding positively, for the most part, to the curriculum modifications she and Jeanette Elk had devised, and she was slowly making friends with one or two of the other teachers. There had been a few upsetting incidents: one of the junior girls announced she was pregnant and dropping out, and one of her tenth-graders had missed a week when his father died in a ranching accident. There had been a few fights, a few kids caught smoking marijuana, a few caught with alcohol on their breath and once the security staff took a knife away from a student. It was all pretty standard fare for a high school, and Shelley had managed her emotional reactions fairly easily. There had been no more sessions spent crying in the teacher's rest room.

At home, there had been no small incidents to mar the improvement in how she felt. She had been surprised at the difference in their relationship that accompanied her initial small effort to face the feelings Blue roused. She found that by focusing her attention completely in the moment at hand, she was able to allow herself more positive feelings without diving into the negative emotions that had plagued her so. A time or two, when Blue had been particularly intense in his lovemaking, she'd been able to open up to him and match his involvement. Her ability to feel the joy and passion between them was growing. On the occasions when she had tried to open her heart to positive emotions and found anger and grief still there, she'd managed to avoid becoming overwhelmed. She imagined the Big Dipper and thought about the star in the middle that had gone out. She thought about what might lay through that gateway. It had calmed her, though she didn't understand exactly why. For the time being, it worked, and that was enough.

Blue had responded happily to her attempts to open up emotionally, displaying more of a teasing, silly sense of humor than she'd seen before. While he'd always been good-natured, now he came home every day with jokes, urban myths and puns he found on the Internet. Almost all of them were new to Shelley, and he made the most of her willing audience. She couldn't remember a one of them to save her life, but she enjoyed them thoroughly when he relayed them.

Every night, they made love, and every night, Shelley learned something she had forgotten about lovemaking. One night, when they inadvertently ran out of Blue's regular brand of condoms and he resorted to a box of novelty condoms one of his brothers had sent as a wedding gift, she learned to laugh again during lovemaking. Another night, after an away cross-county meet that had worn Blue out more than usual, she had learned again to take the initiative and be the more active lover.

Some of what Shelley learned had more to do with trust, however. She was able to hold her full attention with him for longer and longer periods of time as her trust grew. She began to trust that she didn't have to automatically slide into rage or despair at the first sign of any feeling at all. She was learning that she did have some measure of control over her feelings.

The image of the gateway in the sky helped.

For the first time in four years, Shelley felt hopeful about her life, and it was a grand, giddy feeling that shook inside her like the last cottonwood leaves rattling on their branches. Praying trees, Blue said they were called, for when even the slightest breeze moved through them they set up a sweet rustling like many voices offering prayers. Shelley found herself looking forward to the spring when the cottonwoods would sprout new leaves, and the summer beyond when she could walk along the track north of the house and listen to their leaves lifting murmured prayers on the wind.

For the first time in longer than she could remember, she had looked forward to something as normal as a change of season.

It was the first time she realized she was considering staying in South Dakota.

She drove home in a good mood, thinking about what to make for dinner, wondering what silliness Blue would bring home with him today. Maybe she would call her parents tonight.

When she got out of the car, she stopped, instantly aware that something was wrong. Usually the silence was broken only by the wind and occasionally by the horses' calls and plodding hooves in the nearby corral.

This evening, plaintive wails filled the air, heart-stopping cries that Shelley recognized at once. Grief. Inconsolable, wrenching grief.

Her good mood vanished. The sound coursed through her, unraveling the threads in the fabric of a normal life she had thought she was spinning.

Breathe, she commanded herself.

Air rushed into her lungs. She held it a few seconds.

Release. Out whooshed the air.

The wailing continued.

Shelley deliberately conjured the image of the Big Dipper in her mind. In and out, she breathed, staring at the center of the bowl. In and out. In and out.

She calmed enough to realize animals were making the noise. Looking around, she saw Jewel and Crunch at the fence of the corral, nervously watching a herd of milling cattle bunched at the far end of the east field. They belonged to Butch Saltzer, the rancher who leased Melvin Heber's land and another house about a half mile away. The wailing was coming from the cattle.

Something was wrong, but Shelley didn't know what. She wondered if she should call someone, but she knew if she could hear the cattle, Butch and his wife could hear them, too. Clutching her books to her chest, she walked until she stood near the horses. Jewel nickered softly to her, a worried sound, while Crunch tossed his mane and huffed.

"What's wrong over there?" She knew the horses wouldn't answer, but it made her feel better to ask. "What happened to those cows?"

She watched and listened until she couldn't stand it any longer. Inside the house, if she turned on some music, she wouldn't be able to hear them.

It didn't matter. The sound of the crying cattle stayed with her even when she couldn't hear them. She was almost frantic by the time Blue arrived home.

She met him at the door. "What's wrong with them?"

Blue moved quickly to her side. "Who? What's wrong, Shelley?"

"The cows! Didn't you hear them?"

A blank look was her only response.

"Over there." She pointed to the east. "Go back out and listen. Something's wrong."

He stuck his head back out the door, and Shelley heard them again, the sad, mournful cries lodging in her heart, making her want to cry with them.

When Blue came in and pulled the door shut behind him with a rattle, Shelley could see that he was trying not to laugh.

"What's so funny? Something's wrong with those cows!"

He dropped his gym bag and hung his coat in the entry. "It's November. Butch must have shipped the calves today."

"Shipped them where?" As soon as she asked, she knew. They had been sold and shipped to feed lots, from which they would eventually be sent to slaughter. The thought brought the tears she had been fighting coursing down her cheeks.

"Hey, don't cry." Blue tried to take her in his arms, but she held him away from her with one arm extended. "They miss their babies, that's all. They'll be fine in a few days."

"How do you know?" Her voice rose, more with anger than grief. "How do you know they'll be fine? What if they aren't? Then what will happen?"

Emotions flashed in wildfire succession across his face. "Shelley." He used a low, harsh voice she hadn't heard before. "Stop it. They're cattle. I wasn't talking about you."

"I can't stop it. Don't you see? I can't stop it. I hear them crying and I can't stop it." The tears flowed freely, and she tried to stop, she tried to breathe and to calm down. It was just so hard.

Blue reached for her again, placing his hands on her arms. "Yes, you can. Come on, Shelley. Cry if you need to, but don't torture yourself." Resolutely, he drew her to him, refusing to be shut out, refusing to be pushed away.

She let him hold her, and she let herself cry, feeling like an absolute fool. When Blue sighed, she felt worse, knowing that he was frustrated with her, knowing that he wanted to help and neither of them could figure out what she needed.

It took a few minutes, but Shelley was finally able to think of the dipper again, and the invisible star. Shelley imagined angels coming in and out of the middle of the dipper. When they heard the cattle crying, she saw them drift down to the field and walk among them, touching their broad backs, scratching their huge heads, hugging them as Blue was hugging her, whispering that everything would be all right. The cattle still cried, but they leaned into the angels and took comfort in their care—just as Shelley leaned into Blue and took comfort in his care.

Gradually, she calmed, resting her head on Blue's shoulder. The tears dried up, and she closed her eyes.

He gave her a few more minutes. "Okay?" he finally asked.

"I think so." She raised her head and found his gaze wary.

"Want me to make supper?"

"I've already started. Go ahead and take your shower."

He released her to pick up his gym bag again, but she caught his arm as he walked past her.

"Blue?" She wanted to apologize. She wanted to be able to tell him it wouldn't happen again.

"What?"

"I'm sorry. I know I cry too much. I know it doesn't make sense. I should be over crying by now. I want to give you more than tears and constant demands for comfort."

"I want more, too." He sounded frustrated.

"I know." She bowed her head. "There are times when I feel stronger. Almost whole. You make me feel stronger, Blue, and I want to be able to give you what you give me, the support and the care. I've come to care so much about you, and I want to build on that.''

He was silent for a long moment. ''We could build a real marriage.''

As soon as he said it, she realized this was something she, too, wanted, though she had been afraid to hope for it. Yet this afternoon, when she'd imagined what the cottonwoods would look like in the summer, she'd imagined Blue at her side.

''We could.'' She looked up into his eyes. ''You're the best thing that's happened to me in longer than I can remember, Blue. You've touched me.'' She put her fist over her heart. ''You've made me feel alive again.''

''But...'' He said it before she could.

''But I'm not sure I can do it.''

He combed his fingers through his hair and sighed. ''If you keep telling yourself that, you'll never do it.''

''It isn't that simple. This morning I thought I was doing better. On the way home from work, I imagined being here in the summer and I saw myself with you. Then this happened—'' she gestured toward the crying cows ''—and I wonder if I'll ever be capable of a normal relationship. It isn't fair to hold you in the marriage if I can't give you what you need.''

''What do you think I need?''

''Love. A real partner who can give as much as you do.''

''Are you saying you couldn't love me?''

''I don't know if I'll ever be able to love you as well as you would be able to love me.''

''In a marriage, partners give different things in different ways. Don't judge what's fair to me without talking to me about it. I think we could have a good marriage,

Shelley—beyond the end of the school year. We have a solid friendship, and we could have more. Much more. You lie in my arms at night, and you know we've already grown closer than either of us expected we could. But if we're going to have a real marriage, you have to want it, too. You have to want it enough to fight your demons for it. Do you want it that much?''

Shelley was silent for a moment, imagining what it would be like to have a real marriage with this man, one in which she was able to give as he did. "I want to try," she finally said softly. "It might take me awhile."

"I'll wait, Shelley. I'll be here for you. But I need some hope, too. I need to know you're going to try. Is what we have worth working on, or isn't it?"

"Yes. It is. You're worth it. You make trying worth it. No matter how awful I feel, how out of control, how frightened or exposed, you're worth it. That's never been the issue. But I feel as though there's something missing in me, something that binds up my love and ability to give. What if I can't get it back? I don't want to promise something I may not be able to give you."

"There are no sure things in life, Shelley. I'm a grown man and I know that. Do you want our marriage to be more than a convenience? You know what I want."

She took a deep breath. "I want our marriage to be more than an arrangement. I want to try."

"Don't just try. Make it happen with me." His eyes were fierce.

"I'll..." she began. "I will."

He kissed her full on the mouth, then let her go. As he left, though, she heard him sigh.

Chapter Thirteen

The next day, March County hosted a cross-country meet for the high schools from Todd County, Shannon County and Martin. Some of the events began before school was officially over because it got dark so early this late in the season, but Bethany was scheduled to run a five-thousand-meter race at three-thirty. She'd already qualified for the state finals in the ten thousand meters, her best event. Blue wanted her to qualify in the five thousand, as well, so she could show the college coaches who would be present at the state meet what she could do. Shelley planned to be there, mostly for Bethany, but also because she didn't want to go back to the house where the cattle had still been bawling this morning.

She hadn't been able to shake the edgy feeling their crying gave her, and it had been the hardest day in weeks. The students had been restless and fractious. A disagreement in first period had escalated into a shouting match between two students. Second period, half of the group presenting that day had been absent, the remaining members pleading for an extension, everyone else insisting they go ahead anyway. There had been a fight in the cafeteria during lunch, and Bethany hadn't been in class that morning. She'd popped in after lunch to let Shelley know she was going to run. When Shelley asked why she'd missed class, the girl had raced off without answering. The shuttered look in her eyes told Shelley as well as any words could that things weren't going well at home again.

After her last class was finally over, Shelley straightened her desk and gathered everything she needed to take home. She'd run her things out to the car, then walk over to the track where the cross-country courses began and ended. She'd just put her coat on when Bethany came in again.

"Hi! Are you ready? I snuck over here to get you," Bethany said. Her smile was bright, but it didn't mask an odd light in her eyes.

Shelley wondered what was wrong now. "Almost. I was going to take some things out to the car, then come over. You'd better get back out to the track before Blue realizes you're gone."

Bethany hurried to the desk and picked up the pile of books and papers next to Shelley's briefcase. "I'll help you. Is there anything else I can carry?"

"No, I can get it." Shelley held out her arm for the pile. "Go on back to the track."

"No, I have plenty of time, really." She whirled away from Shelley. "Things are running a little late. One of the Pine Ridge kids pulled something warming up. Are you going to read all these books this weekend? Geez, I thought when you got to be a teacher you got to quit reading so much.''

Something was definitely amiss. Shelley caught up with Bethany and put a hand on her arm. ''Bethany, what's wrong?''

The door swung open.

''Hey!'' A tall, thin woman in jeans and a stained yellow sweatshirt launched herself through the door.

Bethany swore. ''I'm sorry, Mrs. Larson,'' she said quickly. ''I didn't think she'd come after me in here.''

With a sinking feeling, Shelley recognized familiar almond eyes and an off-kilter tic to the woman's head that might once have been a saucy tilt. It was Vivian Garreaux, Bethany's mother.

''Get your hands off my kid! Who the hell do you think you are?'' she shouted. ''You aren't allowed to touch my kid!''

Bethany shrank against Shelley, an instinctive recoil, before straightening her shoulders and lifting her chin. Shelley left her hand right where it was. As Bethany's mother advanced into the room, she wanted to back away, but she stayed right beside Bethany.

''Mom, I'm fine. Knock it off.''

''You shut up!'' Vivian Garreaux turned angry eyes on her daughter. ''I told you to stay home today. Why should I have to come all the way here to the school to get you when you know you have work to do at home? I got company coming tonight, that house is a mess and you run off on me!''

As Vivian leaned closer, stabbing a finger in the air in front of Bethany's nose, Shelley could smell the sour, unwashed odor of her body and the faint but unmistakable tang of alcohol. Abruptly, she pulled Bethany back and stepped between her and Vivian.

"That's enough." She didn't recognize the voice as her own. It was as if she were speaking through a thick fog, a fog she wanted to fade into. But she couldn't. She couldn't leave Bethany. "Bethany came to school today, where she is required to be by law."

"You stay out of this! I told you to get your hands off my kid, and you'd better do it now or I'm going to sue you." Vivian was shouting in her face, so close Shelley could see the bloodshot rays fanning out from the other woman's pupils, could feel the unhealthy wash of her breath, as well as smell the alcohol.

The numbing fog receded as adrenaline flooded her system. With it came the rage Shelley tried so hard to deny. Her muscles twitched, and the fingernails of her free hand dug into her palm. More than anything, she wanted to push Vivian Garreaux out the door with both hands, hard. She didn't, but she held her eye as she spoke to Bethany.

"Go get Blue. Now."

Bethany pulled away and bolted for the door, ducking to evade her mother's wild grab. When Bethany eluded her, Vivian grabbed Shelley by the arm, her long nails sinking into the soft flesh of her upper arm. Shelley was so startled, she didn't register any pain.

"You run now, girl, I'm going to beat this teacher to a pulp before you get back!"

Bethany halted and turned.

"Bethany, go!" Even though Vivian was strong, she was also drunk. "She'll end up in jail if she does. She won't do it."

Before Bethany could flee, Vivian let go of Shelley and swooped down on her daughter, grabbing the girl's wrist and giving it a vicious yank. Bethany's other arm came up defensively between them, her hand fisted, poised as if to deliver a blow.

They stood that way, frozen in a violent tableau, and Shelley felt her heart stop. Rage, righteous indignation and keening sorrow poured through her, igniting every cell with an imperative to do something, anything to stop this violence once and for all. Yet she didn't know what to do.

"Are you gonna come with me?" Vivian shook Bethany's wrist again, then cocked her head back toward Shelley. "Your teacher's going to be sorry if you don't."

Bethany lowered her fist an inch at the threat.

"She can't hurt me," Shelley said, trying to keep the quaver out of her voice. "You don't have to go."

"I'll hurt her bad," Vivian promised.

Bethany looked back and forth between them, her breath coming hard and fast.

"I'll get you help. She won't hurt anyone." Shelley held out a hand.

"You remember that girl Danny took to the stock show two years ago?"

Bethany blanched, then cast Shelley a helpless look. "I gotta go," she whispered.

Vivian laughed hoarsely as she pushed Bethany ahead of her down the hall. Tossing a malevolent look over her shoulder, she spit in Shelley's direction. "You leave my girl alone. I'm having her transferred out of your class. You keep away from her, or you'll be sorry."

Shelley didn't follow, sure that if she did, Bethany would pay that much more as soon as her mother had her alone. And she knew she had to call someone now, while she was still moving. The temptation to curl into a protective ball and close out the awful scene was strong, but that wouldn't help Bethany. She had to tell someone what had happened, find the principal, call the police. She scrabbled through her purse for her keys, in case no one was in the school office where the phones were, then ran down the hall.

When she reached the school office, however, she ran right past it and out the door at the end of the corridor.

She didn't think—she just ran, and she didn't stop until she reached the track and the only person she could face: Blue.

"Where's Garreaux?" Blue shouted for the third time, searching the field for Bethany. He couldn't wait any longer. All the other runners were lined up at the start line, and the sun was sinking fast toward the horizon.

Squinting into the sun, he saw a woman running toward the track, a woman in a dress wearing shoes that made her stumble over the tufts of dry grass in the field. Then he recognized Shelley.

Shelley never ran.

"Carl." Blue motioned to one of the assistant coaches. "Get this race started." He handed over his clipboard, then jogged out to meet Shelley without a backward glance.

They met at the edge of the athletic field that bordered the track. Her face was chalk white, eyes as wide as a prairie moon, her chest rising and falling in labored breaths.

"What happened?" He reached for her hands. They were cold.

"Vivian Garreaux was here. She took Bethany." Shelley was trembling. "I have to do something."

Her hair was mussed, and her pallor made him worry that she might be in shock. "Are you hurt?"

"No, I'm just furious." She waved a hand in the direction of the parking lot. "She's going to hurt Bethany."

"Shelley, did she hurt you?"

"No! She grabbed my arm. I'm fine. We have to do something so she can't hurt Bethany again."

Blue heard the race start behind him and glanced back. He had to let someone know he was leaving. "Hang on two seconds."

She nodded. When he let go of her hands, she crossed her arms over her middle and held herself, looking anxiously toward the parking lot.

She hadn't moved a muscle when he returned a few moments later. "Come on. We need to see Steve."

"We should call the police. And social services."

"Yeah. Steve will do it if he's still here." They walked quickly back to the school, Shelley almost jogging to keep up with him.

Outside the office door, he paused. She looked as though at any second she might drop into that cold, distant place where she hid from him and everything else that made her feel anything. "Are you sure you can handle this?"

"Yes." Her answer was strong. "Bethany needs help. Hurry."

She opened the door herself and went in.

Blue stood close beside her while she told the secretary, Linda Lee, and the principal, Steve Skillman, what had happened. He kept one hand in the middle of her back, though he wasn't sure she was aware of his touch. Through the heavy material of her coat, he could feel her heart pounding, and he knew that she wasn't as calm as she sounded. She was probably functioning on adrenaline now. He tried not to think about how she would react when it had run its course.

Jim Brink from the tribal police was already in Gilbert and got to the high school before Steve was off the phone with social services. Within a few minutes of Officer Brink's arrival, Marilyn Tall Feather walked through the door with a young woman she introduced as Rachel Tom. Seated now in Steve's office, Shelley painstakingly told them what had happened, repeating her concern for Bethany's well-being.

During the long interview, Blue's hand never left her back, not even when Shelley told about the threats Vivian had made and he was so angry he wanted to punch a hole in the wall.

"Vivian Garreaux doesn't have a history of beating up anyone but her daughter," Brink told them. "We've had complaints of threats before, but never anything more."

"Bethany believes she'll do more," Blue said.

"Bethany's been on the wrong end of her mother's temper all her life," Brink replied.

"What about the girl who went to the stock show with Danny?" Shelley asked in a small voice.

"I don't know her," Brink said.

Marilyn interrupted. "That would be Damona Little Bear. She used to go out with Danny Strike, one of Vivian's boyfriends. A couple of years ago, she took some drugs that had been cut with dangerous additives. She has some brain damage now."

Brink nodded. "I remember." He gave Shelley a reassuring pat on the hand. "Vivian probably told Bethany some story, claiming she beat up Damona or something. Vivian's in bad shape, Ms. Mathews, but she's not going to hurt you."

Blue promised himself that Vivian Garreaux would be extremely sorry if she ever came within a hundred yards of Shelley again.

"What about charges?" the policeman asked. "We can bring Vivian in on a battery charge."

"Will that make things better or worse for Bethany?" Shelley clutched her hands tightly in her lap while she looked from Brink to Marilyn.

"Kind of hard to predict," Brink said, tapping his pencil on his notebook.

"Can I think about it?"

"I wouldn't think too long. The faster we can get Vivian in front of a judge, the faster we can get her daughter into a safer situation."

"Can't you arrest her for beating Bethany?"

"We'll do our best, Ms. Mathews."

It wasn't until Officer Brink left that a tear spilled from the corner of Shelley's eye. She caught it quickly on her knuckle, and without a word, Marilyn handed her a tissue.

"Can I have a moment alone with Shelley?" Marilyn asked Blue.

"Shelley?" He didn't want to let her out of his sight.

"It's okay." She touched his thigh briefly, a small touch, a wife's reassurance to her husband, but he saw the anguish in her eyes.

If he left, he was afraid of what he might find when he saw her again.

"I'll be fine." There was no conviction in her voice.

He walked out of the room, afraid he was going to lose her. The fear made his chest ache.

In the outer office, he paced back and forth in front of the long counter while Steve, Linda Lee and Rachel discussed what had happened. He was too preoccupied with his own feelings to give them more than half an ear.

She would leave. She would resign her position and leave. She would go back home to her parents where she would be safe, where she wouldn't be constantly confronted with violence and injustice and pain. She would lose herself in a cocoon that would keep the world—and him—at bay.

He didn't want to lose her.

And he knew why.

Damn it all, but he loved her.

All the signs had been there for the past month or so. He'd started to think about what it would be like when Travis and Libby came, and in his visions, Shelley was always there with them. God help him, he'd even caught himself daydreaming about what it would be like to have another baby, a baby with Shelley. He'd imagined her growing round and heavy with their child, and he'd choked up, right there in the computer lab. Then he'd kept himself up that night worrying about how Libby, especially, would handle a new brother or sister.

He'd never breathed a word of it to Shelley. He'd been afraid he would frighten her, that it was too fast.

Now he regretted that. He'd never told her he loved her, and she was probably going to leave him.

He should have known he'd end up loving her. She'd said theirs would be a marriage of convenience, but some part of him had known better from the beginning. Convenience be damned. He'd married her and now he loved her. It had happened a little faster than he'd thought it might, but he'd known from the first time he'd seen her sad smile that he could love her.

Trying to convince himself otherwise, he knew the odds were that she wouldn't stay with him after what had happened today. Jim Brink's insistence that Vivian was no real threat to Shelley aside, he knew the real threat: she wasn't going to be able to endure the terrible anger and the pain, or the grief, or the incapacitating knowledge of her own inability to protect her world from violence and injustice.

If she could just trust him a little bit more, he would do everything he could to make it easier. If she would let him love her, couldn't it help? Hadn't it helped already? If she would just let him love her, try a little bit to love him back, follow where he believed their hearts would take them, if she just gave it a little more time...

He knew better. He knew he couldn't save her. Heaven knew how much he wanted to, but he couldn't. Shelley had to do this on her own, and he was scared to death she wouldn't.

If he couldn't save her, if he couldn't make her love him the way he wanted to, he wasn't going to let her go, either. He just wouldn't. He wouldn't let her hide herself away.

She was his wife, and he loved her. He wasn't going to let her go. No way.

Get a grip, he told himself.

Closing his eyes, hands on canted hips, he tipped his head back to expel a long breath.

"You going to be all right?" Steve asked.

He blinked. "I just hope Shelley will be."

"She does seem kind of fragile," Linda Lee commented. "If you need anything, you just give me a call."

Steve seconded the offer. "If she'd rather not come in on Monday, I understand," he added.

"Thanks."

The door to Steve's office opened, and Shelley and Marilyn came out. Marilyn came straight to Blue.

"I played bridge with your mother last night. She sat in for one of the regulars in my group, and she told me to remind you that you should go out to Verdell's."

His mother. Geez. "Yeah, we were supposed to go out there. We never made it." But it was a good idea.

"You know that I don't support traditional spiritual practices, but Verdell and Kaycee are good people. This might be an excellent time to introduce Shelley to a strong, healthy Lakota family where people take good care of each other." Coming from Marilyn, a dedicated church member who didn't believe in the old ways, the suggestion surprised him. It also carried the weight of an order from the high command. "It wouldn't hurt for Shelley to see that most people on this reservation are not such lost souls. And Blue," she said, touching his arm with one neatly manicured finger, "if you need to, don't hesitate to call me at home this weekend."

Blue shook her hand, touched by her concern for Shelley, who didn't like Marilyn much at all. "Thanks. I will. And thanks for coming this afternoon."

Marilyn and Rachel left then, and Blue went to Shelley's side, one arm slipping immediately around her.

"Marilyn said I should press charges." She didn't look up as she spoke. "It would help get Bethany away from Vivian faster. They have a foster home where she can go, but it's in Sioux Falls."

He kissed her forehead. "You can decide tomorrow. For now we need to get away from here."

"I don't want to go home." At his puzzled look, her face crumpled. "The cows."

Damn. He'd forgotten all about the crying cows.

"Then we won't go home," he whispered, gathering her into his arms.

"I don't know where to go," she whimpered.

"Let me worry about that. I'll take care of you. Everything will be all right. You'll see. Everything will be fine." He turned her face into his shoulder and held her tight, feeling the tremors as she strove for control, and wondering whom he was trying to convince more, Shelley or himself.

Still holding on to her, he picked up the phone on the counter.

"Linda Lee, do you have Verdell Owens's phone number handy?"

He punched in the numbers as the school secretary read them out loud.

Chapter Fourteen

All Shelley had wanted to do when she and Blue finally left the high school was scrunch down deep in her coat and stare out the windshield at the highway. She didn't want to think, and she didn't want to feel anything more. She wanted to let the highway hypnotize her into oblivion.

Instead, Blue had chattered at her like a magpie, telling her about Verdell Owens and his family, asking her questions about her curriculum development work with Jeanette, making suggestions for ways to incorporate computer technology into her classes. If she'd answered at all, she had no idea what she'd said. Now he'd dragged her into a neat two-story house a mile or so east of Wallace, introduced her to at least six people, none of whose names she remembered and left her sitting on a lumpy brown sofa next to a sticky three-year-old determined to share a fistful of raisins with her. She was almost as mad at Blue as she had been at Vivian Garreaux.

No. Not that mad.

But she wasn't happy.

A big man with broad shoulders and a comfortable paunch resting atop an impressive belt buckle poked his head around the partition separating the dining room from the living room. She recognized Verdell from having seen him at the college.

"Junior." He addressed the little boy. "Your mama's got something for you in the kitchen."

"What?" The three-year-old carefully selected a raisin from the lump in his fist and put it in Shelley's lap.

"Macaroni and cheese. And if you eat all your supper, there might be some orange sherbet in Grandma's freezer."

It was sufficient temptation. The child slid off the sofa and galloped into the kitchen.

"Mind some company?" Verdell hooked a thumb in his belt loop and waited for her to answer. His round face held deep smile lines, and casual patience seemed to radiate from him. He was about sixty, she guessed, his graying hair enhancing the image of a strong man relaxing into the wisdom of age and experience.

Shelley shook her head in answer to his query. It was his house, after all.

He ambled in, boot heels sinking in the thick carpet, and sat down on the opposite end of the sofa. "Sounds like you had a pretty rough day."

"Yes."

"Your husband, he's kind of worried about you." Verdell's voice was low and rumbling, the kind of voice a grandfather should have. It created an illusion of security and comfort, one that Shelley readily embraced.

"I know."

"That's good he cares so much for you. It's good to see that kind of love in a marriage."

Shelley stared at Verdell, but she didn't contradict him.

"Your husband thinks it might help if you sweat with us." He chuckled. "I think it might help him, but you can decide what you want to do. I'll tell you a little more about it, if you want."

"I'd like to hear more. Where is Blue?"

"I sent him out with my son-in-law, Cajun." That must have been the redheaded man with the Louisiana drawl. "They're gonna start the fire, get the rocks ready. It'll take a while. I hope you don't mind listening to an old man ramble."

To the contrary, she liked listening to Verdell's voice. "I don't mind."

He made small talk, telling her about his children and grandchildren, relating tales that did indeed seem to ramble. At the end of an hour, however, Shelley realized he'd gotten more out of her in less time than any therapist or counselor ever would have. When he'd mentioned how his oldest daughter, Verlene, had lost her first husband in a riding accident, she had knowingly nodded. After a few gentle comments expressing a father's concern for his grown child, Shelley found herself telling Verdell about Brad's death. It didn't come out all in one piece, but in quiet sentences, spoken in fragments that seemed to fit perfectly between Verdell's words.

At some point, Junior returned in a clean T-shirt and minus the raisins and sticky hands. Verdell scooped his grandson into his lap and kept talking. The boy left after a few minutes, obviously bored with the quiet conversation. Then a pair of older children drifted in, asking if they could put a video on.

"Just keep the sound down," Verdell instructed. "Those are our youngest, Case and Ronnie." Ronnie was a pretty, plump little girl, probably eleven or twelve years old. Her brother Case looked about a year younger. They selected their video companionably, then settled down to watch.

"They're good kids," Verdell said in the same soft voice. "On company manners in your honor, but even when no one's here, they're pretty good." He bragged a little about their accomplishments at school and as pow-wow dancers, and the kids tossed in a comment or two without turning away from the television.

Shelley and Verdell talked until Verdell's wife, Kaycee, called them in to supper.

"It's just soup. You don't want to eat much if you're going to sweat," she explained. Petite, dressed in shorts and a T-shirt even though it was close to freezing outside, Kaycee was at least ten years younger than Verdell. She ladled soup into mismatched bowls and joined them at the table. The dishwasher hummed in the background.

"Maybe I better tell you a little more about the sweat so you can figure out how much to eat," Verdell teased. "Kaycee makes good soup. It's hard to stop once you get started."

"You'll probably want more salt." Kaycee pushed the shaker across the table. "I leave it out 'cause Verdell's supposed to watch his sodium intake."

Shelley sipped her soup. With the addition of some salt, it was still simple, just a little beef in broth with carrots and potatoes, but it tasted wonderful. She hadn't realized she was so hungry. "Is Blue coming in?"

"He and Cajun and the others ate while you two were talking," Kaycee said, shaking pepper into her own bowl.

"Blue told us what happened after school. I thought you might appreciate a little peace and quiet."

"Thank you."

Verdell's eyes twinkled at her over the rim of his coffee mug. "That's why we're going to give her a nice small sweat to get started. Just a handful of us, and only, oh, maybe fifty rocks or so."

"Fifty rocks?" Fifty sizzling-hot rocks in a small enclosure sounded like about forty-five too many to Shelley.

"He's just teasing you," Kaycee said, rolling her eyes. "You know better than that, Verdell Owens. A sweat's a ceremony, not some macho he-man endurance contest."

Verdell pointed his spoon at his wife. "She says that now, but last week she was bragging that over at Donna Bull Bear's place, those old women had sixty rocks."

Shelley didn't like the sound of this.

"You're scaring the girl, old man." Kaycee chuckled. "He does this all the time. Tries to scare people out of his sweat lodge," she told Shelley. "Don't you believe a word he says. Maybe *I* better tell you about the sweat."

They ended up telling her together, finishing each other's sentences, bickering gently when one didn't explain exactly to the other's satisfaction. Before long, Shelley found herself smiling at their teasing and even asking a few questions.

"How many rocks do you really use?"

"Depends," Verdell said. "But it really doesn't matter. If it's a hard sweat, it's a hard sweat, even if you only use a few rocks."

"What makes it hard?"

"You go in there to pray for something. Like tonight, you probably want to pray for Bethany Garreaux, for her protection and safety, for a life for her that will allow her to grow strong and to fulfill all the promise you see in her. It's a big thing to pray for. If you want your prayers to be heard and answered, then you have to put yourself into it. When the water goes on the rocks, you'll feel it. It will draw out the heart of what you want to say. It will draw the sweat from your skin, and it will carry impurities with it. It will draw your spirit, too, and that's the hard part. Body and spirit are one when you sweat. If you have some things in your spirit that you need to get out, sometimes it's hard. Sometimes you have to get them out of the way before you can pray for someone else.''

Shelley knew she had things in her soul that might make it a hard sweat for her, but she did want to pray for Bethany. She wasn't sure she believed in prayers, and she wasn't even sure to whom she might pray, but she was drawn to the idea. When she could do so little else for Bethany, voicing her feelings and concerns in prayer seemed the least she could offer.

''On the other hand,'' Verdell mused, ''sometimes you're ready, and it's not so hard. What do you think, Shelley? Do you want to sweat with us tonight?''

''How many rocks did you say you were going to use?''

Kaycee laughed. ''She's got your number, old man.''

When Verdell joined the laughter, his belly shook a little. ''Oh, not so many tonight. Your husband, he'll be looking out for you. Besides, like I explained, you can leave anytime you need to. You just say *mitakuye oyasin.*''

''*Mitakuye oyasin,*'' Shelley repeated.

All my relatives, it meant, to remind each person that he or she was part of the whole, part of a family that extended beyond the limits of blood and affection that normally demarcated the notion of family. The rocks were relatives, Verdell had told her. The steam was a relative. Each man and woman present in the sweat, and each man and woman present in the world, each one was related to her as part of the whole. Every animal, every tiny bug, every tree, flower and weed, all were relatives. In prayer, she was to remember this and to honor her place in the family of life.

It came to Shelley then that her desire to pull away from everything and everyone to hide inside her own pain was profoundly self-centered. She had been thinking only of herself for a very long time.

Then Blue had come into her life, treating a sham marriage with respect and care, treating her like a real wife, bringing her into his family as naturally as he breathed.

Now there was Bethany, too, a young woman who she could not deny roused fiercely protective feelings in her breast, as well as the more troublesome feelings that she couldn't contain.

Staring at the surface of the knotty-pine table, Shelley acknowledged a level at which she did not want to care about these people. She did not want a family—real, metaphysical or otherwise—that made it impossible to slide into a numbing haze that could not be penetrated by rage or hatred or grief.

Mitakuye oyasin. All my relatives.

Verdell and Kaycee sat with her in silence, their acceptance and support unspoken and unwavering. If Blue brought her to them, then she was welcomed and treated as family. No questions were asked, no conditions laid down. It was a simple gift of such generous proportion it brought tears to Shelley's eyes.

The least she could do to honor that gift was to sweat for Bethany Garreaux.

"I'll go."

Tears streamed down her face, and she didn't even try to stop them. Tonight, there was no need.

Blue and Shelley rode home in silence, tired in body and spirit, yet clear, as well. More than at any time since he'd met her, he knew Shelley was completely present.

Since they had entered the sweat hours ago, something in her had changed. She had cried during most of the ceremony. He had been able to sense all the turbulent feelings she so often strove to conquer and hide. In the absolute dark of the *inipi,* the sweat, she had stopped trying to hold it all in as she came to pray for Bethany. She had accepted her own pain, anger and grief, and not let the emotions stop her from living. Yes, something had shifted in her.

Fear of losing her made him wonder if it would last.

Across the bench seat in the cab, he reached for her, and she unbuckled her seat belt to slide closer to him. His arm went around her, and she laid her head on his shoulder.

He breathed deeply, inhaling the scent of her hair, enjoying the warm press of her breast against his ribs, conscious in his mind that he loved her.

Shelley knew they would make love that night, even though it was late, they were both tired and the day had demanded so much. Maybe that was why. They both needed a final physical release.

But the glow in Blue's eyes when he helped her out of the pickup promised more than physical release, and Shelley knew the sweet vibration between them was about more than sex. Their need to be together tonight was as natural and as pointless to deny as the tears she had shed earlier.

Walking side by side to the door, she remembered what Verdell had said about Blue caring so much about her—that he loved her. Lost in the odd mood that had overcome her after the sweat, she didn't want to think about anything that implied. She was so weary of feeling torn by disparate, seemingly irreconcilable desires. So tonight, instead of worrying about the possibility that Blue might really love her, she smiled to herself.

Key in hand, Blue made a soft, inquiring noise.

She merely shook her head.

Once inside, she prepared for bed while he took care of Shoonk. When she reached for the frothy negligee she'd ordered after her white flannel wedding night, she let it drape elegantly over her arm. Sheer, lacy, whispering silk that promised decadent pleasures, it was both beautiful and sexy.

She folded it back into the box and slipped into bed naked. Tonight she would meet Blue as she was with no accoutrements, no sweet seductions and with a minimum of the distance she knew he hated.

In the darkness, she waited for him, listening to the small sounds he made as he moved through the house. When he came to her, he, too, was naked, his form outlined by the moonlight streaming in from the window.

They shared no words. From the first questing touch, skin to skin, then lip to lip, tongue to tongue and, later, body touching body, there was no room for words, and no need. In the coldest hours of the night, unspoken but not unarticulated love warmed them.

Shelley feared what would happen when that love was spoken. Lying spent in Blue's arms, her breathing slow and even, eyes closed, asleep in all but her deepest mind where she lingered in consciousness to savor a pleasure she had never imagined, much less sought, she found out when he finally whispered into her hair.

"I love you, Shelley." His breath warmed her temple. "I love you so much."

She let him think she was sound asleep, doubting he felt the sudden chill that cooled her limbs.

Why had he had to say it?

There was no disguising her irritable mood the next day. After lying awake for what had seemed like hours, she'd finally dropped off about dawn only to awake before eight when Shoonk stuck his nose in her face.

"Go away!" She pushed him away from the bed. He thought she was playing and made an exuberant hop and bumped into the night table. Shelley just caught the lamp before it teetered over the edge. "Bad dog! Go on! Out!"

Shoonk slunk away. When Shelley sat up and reached for her robe, Blue was in the doorway. For the first time, it bothered her to be naked in front of him. She belted her robe tightly.

His expression was serious. "Are you okay?"

"I'm fine. Shoonk knocked over the lamp."

"I don't think I've ever heard you snap at anyone before." He stepped into the room.

"I'm sorry." He sat beside her on the unmade bed. "I have a headache."

"It's okay. I'm not criticizing. I'm just surprised." He picked up her hand to trace his fingers over the back of it.

She snatched her hand back. Why did he always have to get so close? He was always touching her.

"Something *is* wrong." He dropped his hand to his thigh.

"No." But she said it too fast.

"Shelley, please. Last night we didn't have anything between us. Whatever it is, you can trust me with it."

Not this. Not telling him not to love her. Not telling him she couldn't love him back.

She looked at him, and saw once more how beautiful he was. Dark eyes regarded her evenly, but she could see—no, *feel*—the depth of emotion in him. He was so kind and so good to her, and she was so sick of it she could hardly stand it.

She should tell him something, and she didn't want to lie. There had never been lies between them.

"Last night is what's wrong."

"The sweat?"

"No. Us. Afterward."

"I thought it was wonderful." It was a statement. It was the truth.

"It was, but…" She didn't want to have this conversation. "Things have gone so fast. It makes me uncomfortable."

"What do you mean by 'uncomfortable'?"

"You know." It was hard to talk so directly after having skirted her thoughts and feelings for so long.

"Tell me again."

"Sometimes I feel overwhelmed. There's too much feeling. One thing leads to another, and suddenly I'm so angry I can hardly see straight, or I can't stop crying, or I think I'm going to go crazy."

"Did you feel that way yesterday after you saw Vivian?"

"Yes."

"But you got through it. You were angry and you cried, but you didn't go crazy."

"No, I guess I didn't. But I didn't think I could stand it."

"Shelley, there are always people here to help."

She had learned that last night. "I know. But it's still hard. It doesn't all get better because one day I managed not to lose my mind."

"Or get lost inside your mind."

He understood her far too well. "I don't feel strong, Blue. I don't want to face the things you make me feel."

"What do I make you feel?"

"Overwhelmed." Not good enough. Not able to give enough. Not able to love the way he deserved to be loved.

"So I make you uncomfortable." Irritation crept into his voice.

"Sometimes." It came out very softly.

"When we make love? I thought we'd gotten past that."

"Maybe I haven't."

"Last night you weren't uncomfortable when we made love." There was an unmistakable challenge in his statement.

She didn't contradict him.

"But somehow I made you feel overwhelmed," he continued. "Shelley, we were more in tune with each other last night than we've ever been, and you can't tell me you weren't right with me all the way. You kissed me, you touched me in places I've never wanted another woman to touch, and you laughed and cried when you took me into your body. When were you overwhelmed? When?"

His intensity was too much. She started to pull away, to rise, but he caught her wrist and held her beside him.

"When?" he demanded. "What did I do? Everything we did, we did together. What did I do?"

"You didn't do anything!" She tried to jerk her wrist away from him, but he held her firmly. "It was what you said."

Chapter Fifteen

He had only said one thing. Comprehension flickered hot in his eyes, and he released her abruptly.

"You weren't asleep."

"No."

He released a slow breath, then squeezed his eyes shut. "It upsets you so much that I love you?"

"Blue, please. Don't do this."

"Don't do what? Tell you I love you? Or don't love you? What difference should the words make? When we made love last night, I told you in a hundred different ways that I loved you. You felt it, and you weren't scared then. What difference should the words make?"

"You weren't supposed to love me," she said.

"Things don't always work out according to what we're supposed to do."

"I know." She stared at nothing. "I want to be able to love you, too."

"You don't."

She didn't answer. Why was he doing this, making it worse this way?

"Some people only love once. Did you use up all your love, Shelley?"

"Maybe I did."

The tight line of his mouth said he didn't buy that as an excuse. "Why do you think you can't love me?"

"I just want to run and hide so much of the time. How can I love anyone when I can't even face myself? Blue, I've got this cold place inside me that nothing seems to touch."

"That cold place has warmed up a lot since I met you. The woman I made love with last night didn't have to talk herself into letting me touch her the way the woman I shared my wedding night with did."

So he'd known how hard that had been for her. "I'm the same woman."

"Yes. But you're changing. That's what you said you wanted, wasn't it? Change. And a Plan with a capital *P*."

Some plan. She'd simply fallen into a marriage to a man who thought he loved her. "I think I lost the capital *P* somewhere."

He gave her an unhappy smile. "I think I lost my heart."

He wasn't going to make this easy. She took his hand in both of hers. "I want to love you, Blue. At least in some ways. But if I love you," she said very slowly, "what will I do if I lose you? I can't do it again."

"I don't want to lose you, either."

They sat once more in silence. This time Shelley used the silence to build a wall of distance inside herself, reminding herself that nothing was worth repeating the past four years. She would kill herself before she'd lose like that again.

At length, Blue raised her hands to his and kissed them in a familiar gesture, but his eyes were shuttered. "All right. I'll back off. I won't tell you I love you, and I won't look for you to love me. Will you do one thing for me? When you start to feel overwhelmed, will you tell me about it? Tell me how you feel, what makes you feel that way. I don't want to upset you again. If you'll tell me, I'll know what not to do. Can you do that?"

"I'll try."

"That's all I ask." He rose. "I'm going out to work in the barn."

As he left her, Shelley noticed an uncharacteristic stoop to his shoulders. She was surprised how much seeing it hurt.

Noon came and went, and Blue hadn't come back in. From her seat at the kitchen table, where she was grading topic statements for her students' first solo research papers, she had seen him saddle Crunch and ride off. When he'd returned, he'd driven in to town, presumably to get the mail. He was back now and still in the barn.

Shelley wondered how much there was to do in there. It wasn't even really a barn, just a large shed with four horse stalls divided by an open area fitted out with a workbench.

If he wanted to stay out there all day, that was his business. Looking back down at the stacks of papers before her, she picked up the third period set and was soon absorbed in making comments and suggestions to help students refine their topics.

Halfway though the stack, she came upon Bethany's topic statement. It was handwritten on a sheet ripped from a spiral notebook, one tattered strip of paper hanging from the bottom edge. Her script looked like that of so many adolescent girls, full of loops, big and bold, circles dotting every *i*. Shelley read the title: "Traditional Lakota Attitudes about Children."

She scanned the page.

> Historically speaking, there isn't much evidence of abuse in Lakota families until reservation times. I would like to find out about the values and beliefs that used to protect children from abuse.

Shelley stared at the paper, but what she saw was Bethany, her fist raised to her mother, ready to replay the cycle of violence and abuse in a desperate bid for change, only to be stopped by her mother's manipulative fury.

Rage roiled up inside her. With one sweep of her arm, she knocked the papers to the floor, then stared at what she had done, appalled.

Another vision filled her mind, that of a boy just Bethany's age, the one who had killed Brad. She had seen his shame and his remorse whenever he'd looked at her during his trial, but her heart had been cold. It was still cold, and even after four years she had not a scrap of mercy for him. She hated him now as much as she ever had.

She wanted to knock the chairs over, put her fist through the cheap paneling that covered the walls. She wanted to scream, to run, to get away from this awful desire to express her anger in destruction. It was too much, and she wasn't controlling it. The rage had her. It had overwhelmed her at last.

Overwhelmed. Blue had said to talk to him when she felt overwhelmed. This probably wasn't what he'd meant, but she didn't care. If she didn't do something, she was going to lose it, she was sure.

Desperation drove her out of the house, toward the barn. She found Blue seated at a makeshift desk, a portable computer before him. The violent sounds of a raucous computer game covered the sound of her entrance.

The pretend gunfire and explosions only made her more furious.

"Turn that off!"

Blue spun on the seat of a broken chair that had no back. As soon as he saw her, he flipped the keys to silence the game.

"I'm sorry. I didn't mean to yell at you. I came because you said..." She felt foolish now, stupid and angry, irrational and out of control.

For once Blue didn't come to her, didn't try to touch her.

"You said to talk to you when I felt overwhelmed."

"What happened?"

She paced in the open area between the stalls. "I'm so angry I don't know what to do. I want to just hit something, or someone." She gestured in tight, jerky movements.

"What's wrong, Shelley?"

"I was grading papers and I found Bethany's. She wants to do her research paper on Lakota values and beliefs about children. She wants to find out what happened to a belief system that protected children from abuse." Her voice cracked, but she didn't stop. "All I can think about is how when her mother grabbed her to force her out of my classroom, Bethany raised her fist like she was going to hit her back. She didn't." Shelley stopped and stared at the floor. "Someday she will."

When she looked up at Blue, she saw her frustration and her rage reflected in his face.

"It makes me so mad, I want to do something terrible. I want to find Vivian Garreaux and push her around the way she pushes Bethany around. But it wouldn't help. I'm furious and there's nothing I can do!"

"It *should* make you mad, Shelley."

"But I can't stop it. I can't change anything!" She was shouting, screaming almost, and she couldn't stop. "Parents abuse their children, then the children turn to violence. It just goes on and on. People's lives are destroyed, and no one learns anything. On and on it goes. I hate it!"

"I don't think Bethany's going to become abusive." Blue leaned forward, as though he wanted to come to her, but held himself back. "She'll probably leave and never come back here, but I don't think she'll do what her mother's done."

"You think not?" she asked in a scathing tone. "She's already drinking and smoking pot. She's headed down the same path to substance abuse her mother probably took when she was her age. She has a much older boyfriend, and you can bet he isn't a model citizen, dating a fifteen-year-old. Leaving here won't change anything. She can find drugs and alcohol and men who want to use her anywhere on earth. And when she wakes up one morning broke, her boyfriend gone, a child she didn't plan on crying for toys she can't afford, all her dreams and all her promise gone, then we'll see if she's going to throw that punch."

Blue wasn't so much of a Pollyanna that he needed to argue with her. "It might happen that way, Shelley. But it won't help Bethany if you condemn her before she's had a chance. I saw Marilyn at the post office, and she said Bethany's going to that foster home in Sioux Falls today. She said it's a really good placement.''

"I hope it works." With a flash of pessimistic insight, she knew it wouldn't. Bethany would be back. "But it doesn't matter if it's Bethany, or a million other kids like her. Someone hurts them, and eventually they hurt someone else. Always. They lash out, they don't think and, before they know it, someone's dead." She slammed the flat of her hand against the side of an empty stall.

Blue did stand up then, but he didn't approach her. "Who, Shelley? Who lashed out? Who didn't think?"

Her shoulders shook and her hands trembled, but her eyes were dry. Finally, it seemed, there were no tears left in her.

"Emilio Ossario." The syllables fell like stones from her lips. She had never said his name out loud.

"What did he do?"

She didn't want to say it, even when she understood that this was why she'd come to Blue, to tell him this, to make this confession.

"He killed Brad." She forced the words out, and they sounded low and harsh in her head. "His mother was an addict who left him alone on the streets. He saw the gangs as a way to have some semblance of family. When the gang said 'prove yourself' and the older boys put a gun in his hand, he did."

"I'm sorry, Shelley."

Cold, bitter laughter mocked his compassion, mocked the same inadequate words he'd offered when she'd first told him about losing Brad.

"There's more, though. I didn't tell you everything before. I've never told anyone, but you have to know, Blue. You have to know so you'll understand."

"Why you can't love me?" It was his turn to sound bitter.

"So you can understand that some things will never be right inside me. So you can understand what I lost." She held her fist over her heart. "Here."

Taut lines appeared around his mouth, but he didn't interrupt.

"That boy, Emilio." She said his name with difficulty. "He was tried as an adult because he had a long list of prior arrests, including assault and one attempted murder charge. There was a lot of press about the whole thing, and the D.A. thought it would send a message to the gangs if he—Emilio—was tried as an adult. Anyway, I went to the trial. I didn't want to, but the attorneys thought the jury needed to see me, to see that there was a real person left suffering for what that boy had done. It was over a year after the shooting, and I hated going there, reliving everything that had happened. And I hated seeing him there. The boy. Emilio."

She remembered the numbing fog she had lost herself in during those awful days. It must have started before that, but she didn't think it had been quite so strong, the need to slip away from what was going on around her.

"Every day he looked at me with tears and regret in his eyes. I could see that he felt terrible about what he'd done, and not just because of what it was costing him. He was so sorry. He was sorry he'd killed Brad, and sorry he'd destroyed my life.

"After he was convicted and sentenced, he wrote me a letter. He begged for my forgiveness. He said he couldn't change what he'd done, that he'd made a terrible mistake, and he hoped I would be able to forgive him someday. He told me about his life, about how he hadn't thought anybody's life mattered very much because his didn't. He said he saw two pictures of me in the news-paper. One was of Brad and me at his medical-school graduation. We were looking at each other, both so happy and proud. The other was from Brad's funeral. Emilio said I looked so different. At the funeral, he wrote, my eyes were empty, as if I had no soul left, and he realized he'd stolen my life. He said,'' she continued, her voice vibrating with anger, ''that he saw love in the first pic-ture. He'd never seen love like that. He thought if I could forgive him, maybe someday he would be able to forgive himself for destroying that.''

She dropped her hand, clenching it into a fist. ''I still hate him, Blue, and I hate what he did, and I cannot forgive him.''

Blue waited.

''I can love a little bit, Blue. With my body. Maybe in other small ways, day-to-day things like asking how your day went, things like that. I do feel something for you. I won't deny that. But there is a very deep, cold place in me that holds nothing but rage and hatred. The closer you get, the more I've been having to see that place for what it is. It feels so deep inside me that I don't think even your love can touch it. I can't forgive, and I can't forget. I can't love all the way anymore, either. And I don't want to love you badly. You deserve so much more than I can give you, Blue.''

She left him standing in the middle of the barn, won-dering how they would ever go on from here.

That night Shelley dreamed of stars and angels. High up in the sky she flew, into the clear night sky, the glit-tering stars all around her. They were singing. Each star had a voice, soft and inexpressibly sweet. Around and around she flew, trying to understand the words to the song surrounding her, around and around, moving ever closer to the bowl of the Big Dipper.

When she reached the star that formed the dipper's outer edge, she met a woman there, a beautiful angel, Shelley thought in her dream. She must be an angel, though Shelley couldn't see her wings. She wore the most beautiful blue robe.

The woman beckoned and Shelley went to her. The singing surged through the sky, lifting in pitch and cadence when the blue woman took her hand. Shelley was led to stand in the center of the dipper, and she could see the outline of a hole covered with some kind of round door.

The woman squeezed her hand, and the door opened slowly. When Shelley started forward, the blue woman held her back and shook her head, raising one hand.

A man stepped into the doorway. He was tall and slender with blond hair and happy blue eyes.

Brad.

It took her a second to recognize him. It had been that long.

When she tried to pull away from the woman to go to him, she was held fast. Brad shook his head, and she understood suddenly that neither of them should pass through the door. He stood on his side, she on hers.

He looked so happy. Contentment radiated from him, an expansion of spirit that seemed to extend beyond the limits of his visible body. Shelley had never seen him thus, not even in their happiest moments together.

They didn't speak, because no words were needed. In the way of dreams, she understood. Communication was not bound by sound waves or visual cues.

Brad was part of another world now, a world where she was not to go, at least for now. She felt his care and his concern for her, and for a second she desperately missed all they had shared. Once more he shook his head, an admonition. He pointed down, and her gaze followed his finger. Far below, she saw the little house, the town of Gilbert to the east of it, scattered lights across a dark plain. The house glowed, visible when no others were.

Shelley shook her head.

Brad nodded, smiling at her with a twinkle in his eye, a gleam that had always meant he knew better than she did. It had infuriated her when he had looked at her like that, all the more so because at least half the time he had been right.

She knew he was right this time, too.

She bowed her head in acquiescence, and suddenly she was aware of strength pouring into her from the blue woman. Like a strong current, it flowed into her body, strengthening her.

When she looked back at Brad, the door was closing. He blew her a kiss and held up one hand in farewell.

She let the blue woman hold her, then carry her back to earth, cradling her like a little girl in her mother's arms.

Shelley opened her eyes with a start, expecting to find the blue-gowned woman leaning over her as she slept. Instead, in the quiet hours of the night, Blue slept peacefully beside her, his breath slow and even, his body warm.

It had been a dream. She didn't remember her dreams very often, but she would remember this one.

Rolling onto her back, Shelley didn't think it was too hard to figure out most of the dream. Brad had been gone a long time, but she was only now accepting that he was no longer part of the world she lived in—except in her memories. It was well past time that she moved on. It was time to find her Plan with a capital *P*.

Blue turned and flung one arm across her, his hand curving naturally over her breast, even in sleep. He had refused to act as if anything had changed between them when he had finally come back to the house that afternoon. He'd talked to her as he always did, and he'd touched her in all the small ways he always did. With his easygoing manner, he'd made her feel churlish for even thinking about sleeping on the sofa.

But they hadn't made love.

Shelley wondered how much longer she was going to be able to stay. She didn't feel she could leave before Blue's custody hearing was over, but they didn't even have a date set for that yet.

It wasn't right for her to stay, not if he loved her, not when she couldn't love him back in kind. She wasn't sure exactly when she would have to go, but she knew any plan she came up with now should take her away from him.

The vision from the dream came back to her, and once more she saw Brad as the door swung closed between them. She wondered what he thought about this marriage she'd entered into with Blue. She thought she would have known if he'd been upset, but after all, it was just a dream.

It didn't really matter. It was just a dream, a way of integrating everything she was going through.

Just the same, the vision lingered.

Chapter Sixteen

Shelley slept late that Sunday morning, and Blue didn't disturb her when he left for an early bike ride. The sky was gray and heavy, the air biting cold with the moisture that might bring snow before the day was over. He needed the ride to work the frustration out of his body, to fill his lungs with the bracing air and to feel the steady pump of his heart delivering blood to his straining muscles.

She was still asleep when he got back. It wasn't until he'd fed the horses and Shoonk, then showered, dressed and started the coffee that he heard the bathroom door snick shut and the shower go on.

She'd glided soundlessly through the kitchen behind him, not even bothering to say good-morning. That was not a positive sign. Staring at the coffee dribbling into the pot, inhaling the dark aroma that normally gave him a sense of well-being, he felt his stomach clench the way it had Friday in Steve Skillman's office.

She was going to leave. It might be soon, or she might wait until spring, but he knew in his gut that she would go.

What could he do to convince her to stay? Whom could he get to help him? Maybe if she spent some more time with Verdell and Kaycee, it would help. She'd seemed to like them, and she'd seemed so much better after talking to them and after the sweat.

Until he'd told her he loved her.

Hands braced on the rim of the sink, he expelled the air from his lungs in noisy defeat. He'd known it was too soon. He'd been so sure she had been asleep. He'd been too full of the knowledge of his love to keep it all in. As a result, he'd really blown it, and now Shelley would feel as though she had to leave because of her misguided notion that staying would somehow be cheating him.

Still and all, Blue couldn't figure out any way to be with her except as he had been. If he loved her, she would just have to get used to it unless she wanted to leave him now. Because of his custody petition, she wouldn't go right away—he didn't think.

It might show him for a fool, but he was pretty sure there was more than that to why she would stay at least a little while longer. No matter what she said, he simply didn't believe she couldn't love him the way he loved her. Maybe she needed a little more time, but she'd come so far. Couldn't she see that being able to tell him about her anger and hatred of the boy who had taken so much from her had been a big step?

Besides, she'd said she loved him some. Those few words had given him hope, and it was hope he clung to while he waited for her to join him for breakfast.

The phone rang just as he heard the bathroom door open. He picked it up.

"Hi, Dad!" It was Libby, and for once she sounded cheerful.

"Hi, punkin. What's up?"

Shelley stepped into the kitchen, her hair still wrapped in a towel, her robe belted tightly at her waist. The somber line of her mouth made his heart sink.

"Libby," he mouthed.

She nodded and went into the bedroom.

"Mom wants to know what are we going to do for Thanksgiving?"

Damn. He'd wanted the kids to come here for a few days before the longer Christmas holiday. Now he wasn't sure that was such a hot idea. "I still need to talk to Shelley about it. I'll call you back this afternoon, and we can discuss it then, okay? How's your algebra coming?"

Libby wasn't so easily sidetracked. "Okay. Grandma wants us to come, too."

"I know, Libby. I just haven't had time to think about it yet."

"Shelley doesn't want us to come, does she?"

Blue could picture his daughter's pointed chin jutting forward and the mutinous pout he was sure graced her features right now. "That isn't what I said."

"You didn't say anything. You're trying to talk around the issue. Since you always wanted us to come at Thanksgiving before you got married again, it's pretty obvious what's going on. Shelley doesn't want us." Anger made her tone harsh.

"Shelley hasn't said one way or the other whether she wants you to come or not. I haven't asked her yet." Blue struggled to tamp down his rising irritation.

"How could you not mention it?" Libby screeched. "Geez, we're only your kids!"

"Libby, that's enough of that tone. Do you want to have a civil conversation, or do you want to talk later?"

"I'm only trying to figure out who's more important to you—me and Travis, or her."

Blue pinched the bridge of his nose and scowled. "I'm not going to dignify that manipulative question with an answer. You met Shelley, and you told me you liked her. What's happened to change that?"

"Nothing," Libby snapped, backing down a bare fraction. "I just miss you, Daddy." She went from sharp to whining in a heartbeat. "Mom said maybe we should go to Lander this year with her to give you and Shelley some space."

Carlene's mother lived in Lander, and Libby didn't get along any better with her than she did with her mother.

"Look, punkin, let me talk to Shelley before you get all upset, okay? She's had a rough couple of days, and there really hasn't been a good time for us to talk."

"Such a delicate flower." Libby was back to caustic.

"The mother of one of her students came to school drunk and assaulted her," Blue snapped back.

A small noise alerted him that he was not alone. When he looked up, Shelley stood in the entryway between the living room and the kitchen, an unreadable expression on her face.

"Oh." Libby was instantly contrite. Heaven help him in dealing with her lightning mood changes. "Why didn't you say so? Tell her I'm sorry. Was she hurt?"

Blue didn't comment on the relish he heard in Libby's last question. "No, she's all right physically, but it was an upsetting experience."

"Yeah. Okay. Be sure and ask her today, though, will you?"

"I'll call around four, and we'll work it out then."

After a few more comments, Blue hung up. Shelley stood at the sink sipping from a mug of coffee. He came up behind her, but she stepped away from him when he reached for her.

They stood side by side, looking out the window over the sink, separated by inches that felt like miles.

"It's cloudy this morning," she said.

"We'll probably see snow by evening." It wasn't what he wanted to say. "Still hoping for a blizzard?"

She pressed her lip to the edge of her mug, then lowered it. "No." She sighed. "You were right. It would just be a big hassle. And people might get hurt."

That was what he'd told her last week. He didn't know why it made him so sad to hear her repeat his words.

"Do Libby and Travis always spend Thanksgiving with you?"

He braced his arms on the sink again, sliding one foot forward. "Yeah. Carlene usually drives them to Spearfish, and I pick them up there the day before."

Shelley studied the coffee in her cup intently. "Maybe I should fly home for the holiday."

He gripped the sink a little more tightly. "I thought this was home." If she went, he was afraid she wouldn't come back.

Her eyes met his briefly in a sideways glance. "You know what I mean. It would make my mother happy, anyway."

He straightened. "I'd like you to stay and I'd like to have Travis and Libby come for the long weekend."

"Blue, I..." She put her mug down on the counter. "I'm not sure that's a good idea. What if something like what happened yesterday happens when they're here and I can't control my anger? I don't want to put any of us through that. If I don't think I have it in me to deal with you, what makes you think I can handle your kids?"

"You wouldn't ever hurt them. I know that."

"I'm not worried about hurting them physically. I'm worried about complicating your relationship with them, or making them feel that your home may not always be comfortable for them because of your crazy wife."

"You aren't crazy, Shelley."

"I feel like it sometimes."

He didn't want to argue with her. "You're stronger than you think. You got through Friday, didn't you?" She moved her head in what he took for agreement. "It will help Carlene if we can decide what to do."

"Your children have every right to be with you for the holiday."

There was a finality in her statement he didn't like at all. Hating to ask, he knew he had to. "Will you be here, then?"

She appeared to shrink back into herself. "I don't know." When he turned away, she put a hand on his arm to stay him. "No, Blue, that isn't a fair answer. I don't think I should be. I'm going to call and see if I can't get a ticket to San Diego."

His heart sank like a heavy stone in deep water, a fast, interminable fall. "Shelley, don't." They both knew he was talking about much more than spending Thanksgiving in California. "Don't leave, *mitawin*. I don't want you to leave. Not for Thanksgiving. Not ever."

"I have to leave sometime, Blue. We've always known that."

"No." The force of his denial should make it so.

She kissed him on the cheek, a thoroughly inadequate

apology or expression of regret, and then she walked away. She stopped in the doorway, one foot on the living-room carpet, one still on the faded vinyl of the kitchen. "I'll stay as long as I can, Blue. I'll try to stay until the custody hearing is settled. I'll try. But don't pin any hopes for a long and happy future on me. Please don't."

Ducking her head, she walked into the bedroom and closed the door.

It would take more than a damn door to close him out of her life. He wouldn't let her go as easily as she seemed to hope he would.

The snow began falling late in the afternoon, just before dark. It was a disappointing hail of tiny, dry pellets driven by the cold north wind. Shelley watched it from the porch, wrapped up warm in her coat and gloves. Somehow, she had expected more. She had thought the snow would look as it did at Lake Tahoe when she'd been there for ski trips. Big, fluffy flakes filling the sky with cottony snow, piling up in deep banks, and the snow itself soft and moist, postcard perfect.

This South Dakota snow seemed like an angry cousin to that other snow. It swirled in mean eddies across the hoods of their parked cars and stung her face if she turned into the wind. Stingy accumulations clung to the bottom of the fence and the base of the trees, and the wind swept ceaselessly along, forbidding any semblance of a snowy blanket from covering the prairie.

A long sigh escaped Shelley's lips. In this harsh land, even the earth itself was allowed no mantle with which to hide the winter hardness that had replaced the summer's beauty. Each blade of grass would bear the brunt of winter winds and freezing cold. Long dormant, the life frozen out of each once green and vibrant cell, the grasses now bore silent witness to the long winter to come. Shelley watched with them.

Shoonk appeared on the track winding outside the fence, running madly. When he saw her, he barked and changed course, sailing over the fence in a graceful leap, a last dash across the yard, then up the steps. When he reached her side, he sat and nudged her hand. She absently scratched his ears, and he leaned into her and groaned. He was shameless in his appreciation of her attentions.

Just like his master.

Blue. The thought of him made her restless. Just beyond the periphery of her imagination lurked something that she wanted. She couldn't say just what. To leave this place and live in peace? Maybe, but there was regret in that, a regret she wasn't ready to explore. No, it was something else.

But she had to leave. This wasn't really her life, any more than hiding at her parents' house had been her own. This house, Blue, all of what she had here was a step toward an eventual Plan with a capital *P*. She didn't want to stay here, though. It was too raw, the land itself and the poverty that wounded people all around her. She wasn't strong enough.

The ticket to San Diego should arrive by mail in a few days. She'd bought a round-trip ticket, but she wasn't sure she'd use the return leg.

The next afternoon, Blue stopped by the state social services office after his last class to see Marilyn Tall Feather. She greeted him and ushered him into her office.

"I've contacted my attorney and asked him to see if he can't hold off on the custody hearing until early next year," he announced without preamble. "I wanted to let you know."

"I see." Marilyn gestured toward a chair where he could sit, then folded her hands neatly on her desk. "This is something of a change of heart."

"Don't get me wrong. I want the kids. Badly. But I want something else, too."

"A successful marriage."

"Yeah. Shelley's had kind of a hard time. I'm afraid..." He'd debated the wisdom of telling Marilyn his fears, but she might have some suggestions that would help. Right now he'd take any help he could get to make his marriage last. "I'm afraid she may leave."

"I think you may underestimate your wife," Marilyn said.

"She underestimates herself, I know. But I don't think I'm underestimating how scared she is of herself. She's still dealing with a lot of stuff from the past." He told her more of the details of Shelley's first husband's death, including the trial.

"Ah." Marilyn scratched one manicured nail back and forth on the blotter. "So the situation with Bethany, which has been difficult enough, is also bringing up old fears and grief."

"Yeah." Blue leaned forward. "I need help, Marilyn, and you and Verdell and Kaycee are the closest Turtle Creek has to a therapist. Shelley isn't going to talk to you, and I can't dump her out at Verdell's and say I'll come get her when she's worked everything through."

"What do you want me to do, Blue?"

"Tell me what to expect. Tell me what I can do for her. Tell me how to make it so she won't leave."

"You can't go through this for her, as much as you might want to."

"I know." And he did, he really did, but it was so damn hard to accept. "Can't you at least give me some idea what to expect?"

"Each person handles grief a little differently, and it can be more complicated for people who've been through such a disruptive emotional trauma. But it appears that Shelley is working through her anger over what's happened. When she's done that, she's going to need to cry again, Blue."

"She's been crying a lot."

"Then she's letting go. But she's not done yet. The best thing you can do for her is to allow her whatever she needs to heal." Marilyn gave him a kind but firm look. "She may need to leave for a while, Blue."

"I can't let her leave." The naked desperation in his voice embarrassed him.

Marilyn looked at him as if he were somewhat slow. "She just might come back, you know."

He blinked. Not once had it occurred to him that she might not leave for good. "But how can I know that?"

"You can't. You'll just have to find out if your love entails that level of trust."

Trust. He didn't trust Shelley in this. He didn't trust her to come back to him. What did that say about his love for her? Blue edged back in his chair, making a conscious effort to keep from slouching into it. "I guess that's my challenge in all this, isn't it?"

"I'm sure you're up to it, Blue." Marilyn rose as Blue stood, and her eyes were warm with a restrained smile.

Taking his leave, he hoped she was right.

Chapter Seventeen

Although they hadn't worked together very long, Tuesday afternoons seemed a little empty to Shelley without Bethany. This Tuesday, in the short workweek before Thanksgiving, Shelley decided to occupy herself with preparing a more ambitious dinner than she normally attempted—anything to keep her busy. Tomorrow afternoon she would be driving to Rapid City to spend the night in a motel before taking an early flight to San Diego on Thanksgiving morning.

She didn't know if she'd be coming back.

This might well be her last night with Blue.

The thought brought a wave of relief that she would no longer feel so inadequate in the face of his love. It also brought a measure of regret that she hadn't been up to loving him. He was an extraordinary man. As she had thought before, in another life... In this life, he had been exactly what she'd needed, but he'd quickly outstripped her ability to match his love. Only her promise to stay until he had established joint custody of his children kept her thinking that she might come back at all. She should. If she valued her word, she should return, but she didn't want to.

Staring into the freezer, she removed a pair of rib-eye steaks, then set them to thaw in the microwave. Pushing the buttons on the microwave, she wondered when she'd become so domestic again. She was thinking like a real wife, worrying about Blue's health and planning meals. It had become second nature. That part of living with Blue had been good for her. It had drawn her out of her being so self-absorbed.

That wasn't what she would miss most, however. She would miss Blue. She would miss his easy affection and his sweet kisses. She would miss walking with him in the evenings, and she would miss the stories he shared with her. Most of all, she would miss his love. Even if she couldn't love him the same way, she had never been given a more precious gift.

She was angry with herself for not being able to re-ciprocate that love. It felt wrong to run away from it, but it also felt wrong to stay when she hadn't yet freed herself to love him the way he should be loved.

It was dark by the time she heard Blue's truck rumble down the drive. She slid the steaks under the broiler and went to check her hair in the mirror in the living room. Her face looked pale, her mouth grim. That wasn't how she wanted to greet him. She tried to smile, but it didn't reach her eyes.

Shoonk barked and the door rattled open. In a moment, man and dog burst into the room.

Blue sniffed appreciatively. "Something smells great." Then he looked at her. He froze, one arm half out of his heavy denim jacket, stark emotion glinting in his eyes.

"Hi." She went to him and kissed his cheek, then helped him out of his coat. She didn't want this to be a maudlin affair. "I just put the steaks on. Would you like a glass of wine?"

"Sure." For once, he didn't sound sure, but he followed her into the kitchen and accepted the glass she put in his hand. "It's good," he said after a sip.

He looked around, noting the yellow chrysanthemums on the table, the candles and the two places set as elegantly as possible given their utilitarian housewares. He looked at her, head to toe, and leaned close, scenting her perfume.

Then he straightened his shoulders and lifted her wine from her hand to set both glasses down on the counter. Pulling her into his arms, he kissed her softly, as he so often had in the few months she'd known him. As always, his kiss warmed her. It also intensified the guilt and regret she felt. He was so good to her, and she had so little to offer him in return.

He reached behind her and flipped a CD into the boom box that sat at the back of the counter. The sweet, yearning strains of the Dave Matthews Band's "Crash Into Me" surrounded them, and he pulled Shelley into a slow, rocking dance, holding her head next to his, his lips to her ear.

She thought she would come undone when he tickled her ear with his tongue, but he stopped too soon to whisper in her ear.

"I don't want this to be goodbye." She pulled back, but he held her, one hand at the back of her head, the other wrapped tight around her waist. "Shhh. Just listen. Tonight should be a celebration."

She nodded, her cheek rubbing against his.

"You're my wife." He pulled back to look at her. "I want to celebrate our marriage tonight. Tonight will be about love. Not ideal love, not love as it should be, but love as it is between us. We'll deal with tomorrow when it comes."

For once Shelley didn't argue with him. Still swaying in his embrace, she took his face in her hands and searched his gaze. His eyes were as black as coals, ready to ignite with the fire of his love, full of hope and trepidation, and it hurt Shelley to know that she might disappoint him.

Surely she could give him this tonight. She had told him weeks ago that she would try to make their marriage work. Tonight she had to try. There might not be another chance.

"In another life, I would have loved you for a lifetime," she said.

"Make tonight that lifetime." He spun her in his arms.

She acquiesced with a kiss, one that was not as gentle as his had been. "Tonight, then," she said against his lips.

The smile that broke over his face made him look like an archangel triumphant in glorious crusade. Without breaking the kiss, he swept her into his arms.

"Wait," she gasped.

"No." He was halfway to the bedroom already.

"The steaks."

He backtracked far enough to reach the knobs on the stove and somehow managed to turn everything off and keep kissing her at the same time.

"They'll be ruined," she said, her arms hooked tight around his neck.

He didn't answer, and Shelley didn't need him to, especially not when she hit the bed a moment later, only to have Blue follow her down and arrange himself over her so that she had no doubts about the proof of his love. He gave a deep groan of pleasure.

"I'm going to say it, Shelley." He tugged her sweater free of her waistband and found the silky skin beneath. "And I want to hear it back."

She knew exactly what he meant, and suddenly she wanted to hear it. Arching into the hand that skimmed the underside of her breast, she nodded.

His lips touched hers. "I love you."

This time, she accepted his declaration with only a little fear.

He waited, and she knew what he wanted. He met her gaze unwaveringly. "Tonight…"

"I love you, Blue." It wasn't as easy to say as she wanted it to be, but she felt lighter as soon as she said it. Maybe she didn't love him as well as she wanted to, but she loved him, and it felt good to tell him.

"Say it again," he urged.

She smoothed his hair back with both her hands and smiled softly. "I love you, Blue."

He held her tight and rolled so that she lay atop him, and his chest and belly shook with his pleasure.

"Then show me, *mitawin*. Show me how you love me."

With her hands and mouth, with her eyes and with every rub of her body next to his, Shelley put her heart into her performance. She watched him closely, sensitive to his responses, and what he liked she gave him. If they never made love again, she would have given him this night, and it eased her conscience. It freed her to simply give.

She gave him her mouth with sweet kisses, deep

kisses, tongue-licking, teeth-tickling, belly-lifting kisses
that went on and on. She kissed his nose and his eyebrows and his eyes and his chin. Then she got his ears,
and he squirmed, and she didn't let him go. Down his
neck and up again, into his ear, a tiny bite on his earlobe
and back down to his Adam's apple and the hollow below. She gave him all the kisses she could think of, from
his head to his feet.

She gave him her hands, everywhere, all over his body,
sweeping his shoulders, kneading his back, molding the
firm curves of his bottom, skimming the length of his
rock-hard legs, wiggling his neat little toes. She tugged
at his hair, his earlobes, danced her fingers over his high
cheekbones and down the laugh lines beside his mouth.
Her nails scored his smooth chest, raked his nipples, bur-
rowed under his arms and into his navel. Her palm
cupped him, her fingers traced the length of him, and she
squeezed to feel the sharp pulse of his response.

She gave him her laughter and her smiles. Joy spilled
out in giggles when she hit a sensitive spot under his arm
and he yelped, and when he groaned as she worked her
hand up and down. Laughter bubbled uncontrollably
from deep in her belly when he caught and flipped her,
holding her hands still between them so he could tease
her neck and ears with kisses and licks as she had his.

After arousing them both to the limits of their control,
Shelley gave Blue entrance to her body, and she was
hotter, wetter and more acutely sensitive than she had
ever been. He lay beneath her and she mounted him,
rising up, then sliding him slowly into her. Rocking, lifting, riding him, she gave him everything she had in that
moment. Hands linked, their eyes never wavered from
each other's, and Shelley gave him all the things he'd
always given her.

"You're beautiful," she panted, back arching as their rhythm increased. "You feel so good, so strong and hard." Her breath caught. "I've never felt this way, Blue. I've never wanted anyone the way I want you."

The fire that roared between them was pouring into her muscles, tensing them, goading her heart. Each thrust, each retreat and penetration, moved her closer to release, made her clench his hands more fiercely, ride him harder.

She tumbled first, the spasms pushing him over the brink, as well. They cried out as one, both backs arched, hands bound in an iron grip, and let the pleasure take them.

When she could stand no more, Shelley collapsed onto his chest, her breath still wild, her skin still flaming.

Lifting her head, her lips curved helplessly as tremors, half from laughter, half from tears, shook her.

"I love you, Blue."

Then she kissed away the salty tear that trickled from the corner of his eye.

In the morning, they hardly spoke. When it was time for Blue to go, Shelley walked out to the pickup with him, still uncertain of the future, but knowing more than ever what she would lose if she didn't come back. So much lay at stake. No words seemed adequate.

"I want you to come back," Blue told her.

She didn't want to argue now. "I'll call you from San Diego," she finally said.

Then he kissed her fiercely, as though he'd never let her go.

But he did. "Thank you for last night." The heat in his eyes could have melted the deepest snows.

"Drive safe," she said.

"You, too."

Shelley drank in the sight of him, his dark eyes, the deep creases of his bittersweet smile, and she watched him climb into the truck and drive away. She walked to the porch to watch him eventually disappear over the rise of the section road. The morning air was brisk, too cold to stand outside much longer, but she stayed until the last bit of dust had settled. She raised a hand he couldn't see in farewell.

He hadn't told her he loved her again. She wished he had, and she wished she'd told him that she loved him. After last night, she was coming to understand that Blue truly didn't believe she needed to love him in exactly the same ways he loved her. However flawed her love might be, however limited by fears and by the past, she understood that he needed her and wanted her. She also knew that she wanted to come back, but she still felt fragile, too conscious of wounds that Blue couldn't heal, of the anger and grief that still bound her. Yes, she wanted to come back to Blue, but she had demons left to face, and she was unsure she possessed the strength to defeat them.

Shelley finally went inside and continued packing. She emptied drawers until her suitcase was full and then went to the basement to get boxes for her books and papers. These she packed, taped and labeled, and then it was time to go to school. She could come home during her lunch break to finish. The day before Thanksgiving was pretty much of a formality with so many students off early on holiday travels. No one would miss her.

The day dragged. A little more than half her students were in class, and she'd arranged for a video. By the third time through it, her mind was wandering.

All she had to do was look at Bethany's empty chair in her third period class to know that those hard places were still with her. They hadn't melted in the basking glow of love. They were still there, and she was still angry. Somehow, for a night, she had been able to tap her emotions without rousing this frozen dragon, but how often might she be able to do that? She wanted to come back, but her instincts told her that she wasn't ready to make a final commitment to Blue and to their marriage. If she wasn't able to do that, it might be better not to come back at all.

By the end of the school day, she was no closer to a decision. She'd talked to Steve again, telling him she'd call him on Saturday to let him know what she was going to do. She would stop by the house to finish organizing her things so that Blue could mail them to her easily, and then be on the road while there was still a little daylight left.

The house felt empty when she got there, and her boxes stacked up beside the basement door looked forlorn. Pushing aside this melancholy train of thought, she changed into jeans and a comfortable sweater, then carried the boxes downstairs and took her bags out to her car. Shoonk trailed her from the door to her car, looking at her expectantly.

"You can't go with me, fella." She dropped to one knee to give him a vigorous rub. "You take good care of Blue for me, you hear me?"

Shoonk leaned into her and sighed. She gave him an extra good ear scratching, aware she might never see him or his master again, then dropped a kiss on the top of his head.

One last time, she went into the little house. The glass rattled when she pulled the door closed, a sound she would forever associate with Blue coming home in the evenings.

She wandered through the house, into each room, ostensibly checking to see if she'd left anything. She saw the bed in the spare room covered with a pretty new floral spread for Libby, and the wrapped package the size of several stacked CDs on the pillow. In the office, Blue had made the daybed up for Travis, and there was another wrapped package beside his pillow, as well. She knew it was a computer game, one Blue wanted every bit as badly as Travis did.

She ended up sitting on the bed in her and Blue's bedroom. The light outside was fading, and she needed to leave, but she couldn't quite bring herself to. If she waited too long, Blue might get back with the kids, and that would be awkward. She would leave in just a minute more.

When the minute was up, she reluctantly rose. It was time to go. She might be back, she told herself. She might be back on Sunday night.

But she might not be.

She took a deep breath and thought she detected the faint, lingering scent of Blue's soap and their lovemaking. She held it in her lungs, then turned to leave.

As she swung the door open, the phone rang.

Chapter Eighteen

Shelley debated answering. It was most likely one of Blue's relatives, who could leave a message on the machine.

On the third ring, she pushed the door shut and ran for the phone. She caught it just before the machine was activated, her voice breathless when she answered.

"Hello?"

There was no answer, but Shelley could tell there was someone on the line.

"Hello?" She spoke more briskly.

"Ms. Mathews?" The familiar voice was soft and frightened.

"Bethany?" A chill swept down Shelley's back.

"Yeah. It's me."

"Where are you?"

"My mom's. I need help."

Shelley's heart thudded. "Are you hurt?"

She hesitated, and Shelley knew she was. "I'm scared, Ms. Mathews. She's really mad at me. She locked me in, and I think she went to get a gun. I think she's going to kill me."

"Can you call the police?"

"No! I'm not supposed to be here." Her voice rose hysterically. "They'll put me in a group home or something!"

There was no sense arguing with her now. "All right, calm down. Where's your mother's house?"

Bethany gave her the name of a road in Lodgepole. "It's the green-and-white house, third one on the right. Please hurry."

"I'm coming, Bethany."

"Please." She hung up with a soft click.

Dear God, Shelley thought, this is why I have to leave this place. I can't deal with this. What am I going to do if Bethany's mother really does try to kill her?

Rage surfaced suddenly through her fear, and she knew she wanted to stop Vivian Garreaux from hurting Bethany again as much as she'd ever wanted anything in her life. How dare the woman treat her daughter this way? How *dare* she?

She had to hurry. Glancing at her watch, she saw that Blue really would be home soon, so she took a moment to scrawl a note for him and tape it to the phone. Snatching up her keys and purse, she ran to the car.

It took ten minutes to get to Lodgepole, and five more to find the right street. With the sun almost down, the roads were growing slick with ice by the time Shelley turned onto what she prayed was the right street. It sloped up from the river valley toward a collection of houses laid in neat rows on the crest of a hill. Ahead on the right, Shelley saw two figures in front of a green-and-white house.

Driving faster than she should, she felt the car slide a little on the ice when she pulled to the side. Almost hidden from view by a camper, she saw a small knot of young people watching the scene unfolding before them.

Shelley recognized two of her students among them, Brendan Wilke and a girl from her second-period class.

"You get in that house!" Shelley heard Vivian scream at Bethany. "You get in there or you're gonna be sorry!"

From the street, Shelley couldn't see any sign of the gun Bethany had been afraid her mother might have.

She went first to Brendan's side. The students looked ill at ease with her presence. "Has anyone called the police?" she asked quickly.

Only Brendan looked at her. The others stared at the ground or toward the house. "No," he mumbled.

"Why not?"

"Lots of folks don't like the cops, Ms. Mathews."

She didn't have time to argue. "Will you call Eloise Larson and tell her what's going on here?"

It took Brendan a moment before he nodded.

"Tell her I'm here," she added. Brendan turned to go. "And hurry."

Blue had dreamed for years of the day when he would once again bring his children into his home, a real home with a room for each of them, a big kitchen table to sit around and enough space to play inside on rainy and snowy days. As he made the last turn into the driveway, his heart was both full and empty at the same time; full because Libby and Travis were with him, empty because Shelley was gone.

He'd more than half hoped to see her gray Toyota parked beside the gate. It wasn't there.

He wouldn't think about her now. He had the kids to worry about.

"What do you think?" he asked as they bounced down the rutted driveway.

"I see Crunch!" Travis exclaimed. "Wow—the horses are right by the house."

"It looks very nice." Libby was trying out her grown-up voice. "Kind of isolated, though. What is it, about a mile and a half to town?" She assessed the distance accurately.

"Don't get any ideas," Blue warned as he pulled to a stop.

Travis was out the door immediately. "Can I ride Crunch before supper?" He stopped first to greet Shoonk, then the two of them ran to the corral fence.

"Want to see your room?" He hoped Libby would like it. Knowing she'd want to decorate herself, he hadn't done much more than put in a bed with new linens and a small dresser.

"Sure." She trailed him into the house, looking around her with interest. "You could put flower boxes along the porch and under the windows," she said.

"Maybe you could help next spring."

"You make the boxes, I'll figure out what to put in 'em," she agreed. "Definitely petunias. Red and white ones."

He chuckled, unable to contain his joy at the thought that both his children would be here with him in the spring. Right alongside the pleasure, though, he was unable to ignore the sharp stab he felt wishing Shelley would be, too.

Travis and Shoonk ran up just as Blue got the door

open, and both kids and the dog spilled into the house. Shoonk barked at all the excitement, and Blue followed. "Bedrooms to the left," he called.

Travis went straight back, but Libby took her time, looking first in the living room, then poking her head in his and Shelley's room. Rather, what had been his and Shelley's. Maybe it was just his now.

"Cool!" Travis hollered from the back bedroom. Blue could hear the paper ripping on the gift. "Thanks, Dad. Cool!"

"There's something for you, too. On your bed," Blue told Libby.

His daughter ran a hand over the smooth surface of the big double dresser. Shelley's hair bands and jewelry and the ever present stack of student papers were gone, and the room looked too neat, almost sterile without them.

"Is she coming back?" Libby asked, startling him.

He'd told them Shelley was going to San Diego to be with her parents, but no more. "Why do you ask?"

"There's a stack of boxes addressed to her in San Diego." She pointed.

Blue looked past her to the three cardboard boxes beside the dresser. The finality of Shelley's leaving hit him like a blow to the gut, and he subsided against the door frame.

"Well? Is she coming back or not?"

"Doesn't look like it." He strove for a normal tone, but he wasn't fooling Libby.

She looked disconcerted. "Oh. Do you want her to?"

"Yeah, I want her to."

"Is this a surprise?" She walked back toward him, her arms tucked close to her body and wrapped across her waist in a gesture he'd gotten used to after his divorce.

"No."

"Is it because of us?"

Blue straightened, then pulled his daughter into a big hug. "No, punkin, it hasn't got a thing to do with you. Not one thing. Don't ever think that. Shelley has some things she needs to work out. You remember what she told you about her first husband, and how he was killed?"

Libby nodded against his chest. She was small, like her mother, and despite all her attempts to prove otherwise, she still felt like a little girl in his arms. "I thought that was a really long time ago," she said.

"Sometimes people need a really long time to work through things."

"I'm sorry, Dad."

He was, too. "Thanks, punkin. Want to see your room?"

"Sure."

"Dad!" Travis bellowed. Volume control was something they were going to have to work on. "You better come here. Shelley left a note for you."

Blue and Libby found Travis in the kitchen beside the phone.

"It says something about Bethany and an emergency." Travis's dark brown eyes were round with excitement.

Blue snatched the note and read it in a glance. Bethany was back and in trouble. Shelley had gone to find her and had asked him to follow.

She wasn't gone. Relief surged through him. He looked at the clock and realized that she must have left just minutes before he'd gotten back.

"Guys, we have to drive up to Lodgepole. Go get back in the car and I'll explain when I get there."

"But, Dad—" Libby started.

Blue cut her off. "This is serious. Go. Now," he ordered as he picked up the phone. "I'll be right there."

The kids went, and he punched in the number of the tribal police in Lodgepole.

Standing in the street, Shelley could hear Bethany's and her mother's raised voices. Somehow, Bethany must have gotten out of the house, but not in time to get away. Now Vivian was trying to force her back in.

"If you don't get in there now, girl, I'm going to take everything you left here and burn it up."

"No," Bethany replied, her voice breaking. "I'm not going back in. You can't make me."

"Get inside!" Vivian brandished a fist and Bethany shrank back. "What'd you come back here for anyway? You're nothing but trouble!"

Cautiously, Shelley approached the raging pair. Her stomach knotted and her hands were icy inside her gloves, but she forced herself onward. Bethany saw her, then swung her gaze warily back to her mother, who stood, gesturing wildly, with her back to the street and Shelley. One particularly energetic wave of her arm nearly overbalanced her, and Shelley knew Vivian was more drunk than she had been in their previous meeting.

Having no idea how she was going to stop this scene, Shelley advanced until she was only ten feet from Vivian. Bethany was trapped on the small porch, hemmed in by an aluminum railing. She had pulled a low gate shut, an inadequate barrier to her mother's rage.

From so close, Shelley could now see that Bethany had a rapidly swelling eye and a still bleeding cut on her chin. Her cream-colored sweater was torn at the neck and spotted with blood. The thought that there might be other, less visible injuries sickened Shelley.

It also focused her anger once again. Vivian had to be stopped.

As Shelley moved toward Vivian's back, the woman lunged toward Bethany, pushing her back from the gate with both hands. Bethany staggered but hung on with both hands. She swung the gate out, using it as a ram to force her mother back.

The escalating violence froze Shelley for an instant, and she had to fight an overwhelming urge to curl into a protective huddle and close it out.

In that moment of paralysis, she saw Vivian raise her fist again, and this time it was no mere threat. As if in slow motion, Shelley watched her arm swing back, then arc toward Bethany's face.

"Stop!" she shouted.

But it was too late, and Shelley watched helplessly as Vivian's blow connected with Bethany's jaw.

"Stop it!" She launched herself forward to pull Vivian away, but once again she wasn't quick enough.

Bethany's head snapped back, but she recovered quickly, and when she did, there was fury in her eyes.

"That's it. I don't care if you are my mother, you're never going to touch me again."

Before Shelley could move, Bethany reached for her mother with both hands, grabbed her by her shirt and hauled her over the gate. With a strength fueled by years of suppressed anger and surrender to abuse, Bethany shook her mother, then slammed her into the side of the house. Momentarily stunned, Vivian didn't fight back. Bethany slammed her fist into her mother's face.

"Bethany! No!" Shelley wrenched the gate open to get to her. "Don't do this!"

"Why not?" Bethany screamed back. Her mother dropped to the ground and rolled into a protective ball.

Bethany began kicking her. "She's beat up on me all my life. Now it's your turn," she yelled at her mother. "If I have to kill you to stop you, I will."

Heart pounding, unable to breathe, Shelley wanted to turn and run. She didn't want to see this. She didn't want to see Bethany embrace the violence that had marked her life so brutally. Most of all, as she watched the awful scene before her, she didn't want to remember Emilio Ossario's face. She didn't want to remember his words as he took the stand to tell the court why he had killed Brad Mathews.

The words came back to her all at once, and the violent image of Bethany kicking her mother cut in and out with memories Shelley had thought long-buried.

He had been in trouble, he had said. He'd stolen money from his mother's latest boyfriend, and the man was out to get him. He didn't have anywhere to go, and the guy had connections to some dangerous men. They'd caught him once and beaten him badly, promising that the next time, he wouldn't live through it.

He had needed help. He had needed protection. The young men with the gun had offered it.

Was this the kind of desperation that had driven Emilio Ossario to accept a dare and a gun? Was this the kind of rage that had pushed him into firing into a crowded street?

She hadn't cared.

She cared now. She cared for the girl who had just taken the first step toward violent solutions to terrible problems.

No matter how much it was going to hurt, Shelley knew she couldn't turn away from Bethany.

Her body responded with awkward jerks, but she

closed the space that separated her from Bethany. First she caught Bethany's flailing hands.

She resisted, trying to break Shelley's hold.

"No," Shelley said, pulling her firmly away from Vivian, who lay whimpering on the ground. "Stop, Bethany. She can't hurt you."

Bethany tried to yank free one last time. Then, as quickly as the wildness had claimed her, the angry light left her eyes.

Her face crumpled, and she began to cry.

At the sight of Bethany's tears, Shelley remembered that Emilio had cried when he'd faced her at his trial. She had forgotten that he had cried every time he saw her.

"Oh, God, Ms. Mathews," Bethany sobbed. "What have I done?"

Shelley opened her arms and held Bethany tightly. She couldn't tell the difference between the tremors that shook her body and Bethany's sobs, and it took a while before she realized she was crying, too.

Vivian groaned, and Shelley turned to take Bethany away before anything further happened. Facing them, on the other side of the gate, stood Blue and two Turtle Creek tribal police officers.

Shelley pushed open the gate, keeping one arm tight around Bethany's shoulders.

Blue was at her side in an instant. He wanted to hold her, she could tell, but she didn't let go of Bethany, so he put a hand on her back, as he had that awful day at school. She knew he wouldn't leave her.

"Are you okay?" he asked.

"Yes. Bethany needs to get to the hospital." Her voice was surprisingly strong.

They looked at the officers. "We'll meet you over there when we're done here," one of them said.

"Where are Libby and Travis?"

"At my mom's. She called the police. So did I." He stopped. "We'd better go."

Shelley let him lead them to his pickup, never letting go of Bethany, who clung to her, sobbing still.

And for as long as Bethany cried, so did Shelley.

Chapter Nineteen

Shelley didn't leave Bethany's side. She sat with her in the emergency room at the Indian Health Service Hospital. She held Bethany's hand while the young doctor examined her, stitched the cut on her chin and ordered X rays to make sure there were no broken ribs or internal bleeding. Then she hovered outside the door to the X-ray room.

Blue never left her side. They navigated through the hospital like some sort of three-headed beast. When Bethany went into the X-ray room, he sat down in the deserted waiting area and pulled Shelley onto his lap.

"You're still crying," he said, handing her another tissue. He seemed to have a good supply in his coat pocket.

"I can't seem to stop." She wiped her face again, but with Bethany out of reach for a few minutes, the sobs she'd been keeping under control broke free.

"It hurt so much to watch." She choked the words out between shuddering breaths. "When Bethany hit her mother, I thought I couldn't stand it. I wanted to leave."

"I know."

She knew he was thinking about the day in the barn when she had told him why she couldn't love him. "I could see him, Blue. Emilio Ossario." Her voice broke over his name. "When I looked at Bethany, I saw him." She wanted to say more, but no further words made it through her tears.

Blue cradled her head against his shoulder and rocked her. "Go ahead and cry, *cantesicela.* Cry it all out. There's no one here." He stroked her hair. "Just let it all out."

She did. Shelley cried for Bethany, for herself, for Brad and finally, after so many years, she cried for Emilio Ossario. She cried not just for what he had done wrong, but for the pain and the fear that had driven him, and for all the wasted years of his young life.

She realized he wasn't even twenty yet. He'd received a life sentence. In the past, she had taken comfort from that fact. Now it made her cry all the harder.

And all the while, Blue held and rocked her, saying nothing, simply offering his strength and acceptance of everything she brought to him: all her problems, all her failings, all her sorrows.

It occurred to her that she would be a fool to throw away his love—in this lifetime or in any other.

Gradually, she quieted and simply lay with her head tucked into the curve of his neck, letting the hand he stroked up and down her back calm and soothe her.

"I want to stay with Bethany tonight, if they'll let me," she said when she trusted her voice again.

His hand went still at the bottom of its course. "Does

that mean you aren't going to San Diego?" There was careful hope in his voice.

"To be honest, I hadn't thought that far ahead. I don't think I can answer you right now."

His hand resumed stroking as his chest deflated, and Shelley had the feeling he was trying now to comfort himself as much as her. "What about your flight in the morning?"

"I'll see if I can reschedule it." It would be difficult with the holiday weekend under way. "You should go home with Libby and Travis."

"I don't want to leave you."

"I'll be okay. The kids need you."

There was need in his eyes, as well, but he didn't speak of it. "I'll stay until the cops have talked to Bethany."

The X-ray technician peeked out through a crack in the door. "All clear?"

Shelley realized the young man had probably been keeping Bethany occupied while she cried.

Reluctantly, she slid from Blue's lap. "All clear," she said. "For now."

Late the next morning, she had to say goodbye to Blue again in front of the hospital. They stood awkwardly between her car and his pickup in the parking lot, which was largely deserted because of the holiday.

After a night with no sleep and the morning nearly spent, Bethany had been discharged from the hospital and picked up by her foster parents from Sioux Falls. Shelley had managed to get a seat on an early-afternoon flight, and she needed to get on the road if she was to make it, but neither she nor Blue was anxious to make their farewells again.

"Bethany's lucky the foster family was willing to take

her back," Blue said, clearly trying to delay the inevitable.

"The Martins seem like good people. They were so worried about her. I think she may stay put this time." She was killing time, too, reluctant to say words she knew he didn't want to hear.

"Why did she come back?"

"To see her friends," she said, "and to look for a necklace her grandmother had given her. Her mother hid it because she knew how much it meant to Bethany." Shelley sighed. "I can't imagine treating your own child that way. I can't imagine treating anyone that way."

"Vivian isn't well."

That was an understatement. "Rachel said she was going into a treatment program again."

Blue nodded. "Jim Brink said the cops pulled Vivian's boyfriend over last night for driving under the influence, and they found a gun in the car. Thank God he wasn't around when Vivian was looking for him earlier."

Rachel had passed along the same news early this morning, and as it had then, it made Shelley shudder. "No child should have to live like Bethany has."

"No." Blue wrapped her in his arms, holding her tight. She put her arms around his neck and held on tighter. Cheek to cheek, they stood that way for a long time. Shelley inhaled the scent of his soap, a faint whiff of horse, and Blue. Rubbing a finger over the worn threads of his denim jacket, she closed her eyes and absorbed his warmth and steadfast support. She was so tired she thought she could sleep standing on her feet as long as Blue held her. He would never let her fall.

When at last he spoke, he startled her, rousing her as if from a trance. "You're sure you don't want to come to Regina's for dinner? Maybe take a nap?"

She released her hold on him a fraction. "I need to go. My flight leaves at two." It was almost eleven-thirty and it was a two-and-a-half hour drive to the Rapid City airport.

Blue dropped his hands to her waist so he could look at her. Seeing the plain desire and so much more in his expression, she lowered her head. He tipped her chin back up. Love. That's what the something more was that glowed in his eyes, and underlying it was a vulnerability that staggered Shelley. Once again she was humbled in the face of his love.

"Has anything changed?" he asked her quietly.

She didn't know how to answer. "I think," she answered slowly, not wanting to give him false hope, not wanting to make the fact that she might leave him permanently hurt any more than she could help, "that something is changing. There are some things I need to do in California. Then I'll know. I hope." The pain in his dark eyes nearly undid her. "I wish I could give you more, Blue. I feel as though I've come back to life after a long sleep, like Rip Van Winkle or Sleeping Beauty or something. I don't know who I am anymore. It's been so hard."

"You've handled it. You haven't broken."

"Partly because of your help and support. But there are some things I have to do myself. There are some things you can't help me with, and until I've seen if I can do them, I won't know what to do."

"You're stronger than you think, Shelley."

"But am I strong enough to love you the way you deserve to be loved?"

"Love isn't something to be measured. I'll take whatever love you have to give and be happy. You know that."

She cupped his cheek. "We both know that the best marriages happen when people love in kind. I want the best for both of us, Blue. I don't want to feel guilty, or as though I'm cheating you somehow." She placed a kiss on his cheek. "I'll call you soon."

His lips met hers in a searing kiss that went on and on. Shelley wasn't sure she ever wanted it to be over, but when it was, she stepped quickly away from him.

Her hand on the car door, she took one last look at him. The wind and their embraces had loosened a strand of his hair from his ponytail, and she reached to tuck it behind his ear.

He caught her hand and kissed her fingers.

"I love you, *mitawin*. Never forget that."

"I won't," she said. Then she gave him her best smile. "I love you, too."

Then without another word, she left.

In all his life, Blue didn't think he'd ever been so torn. Between the sheer joy of having his kids with him in his new home and the deep sorrow of Shelley's leaving, he felt like a crazy man. Sorrow wasn't all he felt. There was fear, as well, fear of what his life would be like without her. He'd never loved a woman the way he loved Shelley, and they'd only skimmed the surface of that love. He wanted to explore their love, to grow with it, and he was afraid he wasn't going to get the chance.

Excusing himself from the living room, where several of the adults were watching football and some of his cousins' younger kids were playing a board game, he went through the bustling kitchen and out onto the back deck. Down in the yard, Libby and some of the other girls were playing tag football while Travis and the kids his age were horsing around near the garage. It was a nice afternoon, warm after yesterday's chill.

Blue glanced at his watch and saw that it was a few minutes after two. Shelley's plane would be airborne, climbing high above the Black Hills as she traveled west, away from him.

It didn't take long to get to California by air. If Shelley didn't come back, maybe he ought to go after her. He wasn't going to let her go without a fight. He'd give her a week. Well, maybe a little longer, but if she wasn't back by Christmas, he was going after her. That's all there was to it. A man didn't let the woman he loved walk away without making damn sure he'd done everything in his power to keep her with him.

The back door opened, releasing the holiday aromas of roasting turkey, dressing and pumpkin pies, and his mother came out, something shielded under her sweater. When the door was closed again, she pulled her hand out to reveal a fresh piece of fry bread.

"Here," she said. "I swiped this from your Aunt Janiece. She thinks nobody else knows how to make fry bread but her."

Blue accepted it, then broke it in half to share with his mother. He took a bite. It was good, still warm, yeasty and sweet with raisins. "It's not as good as yours, Ma."

His mother chewed thoughtfully. "I guess it's okay, though," she admitted grudgingly.

They finished the fry bread in silence.

"Libby says your wife isn't coming back." There was no accusation in the words, just a simple statement of fact.

"I'm not sure yet."

"I imagine right about now you're thinking maybe you should go get her."

Blue narrowed his eyes. "How do you do that? I swear, I ought to put you in the circus and charge five dollars to have you read people's minds. I'd be so rich I'd never have to work again."

His mother just smiled. "You try to put an old lady like me in the circus, the social services folks will get after you. You'd be really sorry."

"You forget. I have friends at the department of social services."

Eloise huffed dismissively. "That Marilyn Tall Feather. That woman's meddling got you married in the first place."

Blue wondered what else his mother knew. "I'm not sorry I married Shelley, Ma. I love her."

"But does she love you?"

"I think she does." Innate honesty made him qualify. "I know she loves me some."

"What's some? Either she loves you or she doesn't."

Blue didn't respond. In silence, they watched the touch football game.

"She let him go."

Blue looked questioningly at his mother.

"The other husband. She let him go."

"How do you know?"

"The blue woman told me."

Blue had no idea who the blue woman was, and he didn't bother to ask. His mother was in one of her cryptic moods.

"He was a nice man. Not holding her at all. I think he even approves of you. And she let him go. But she has something else to let go. That's why she had to leave."

"Ma, this is a weird conversation." He looked at her in exasperation.

"She knows what she has to do," Eloise said, ignoring his complaint. "You have to trust her. Let her do what she needs to do."

A shiver ran down his back. "Will she come back?"

Eloise shrugged. "Nobody told me that. You just have to wait and see."

"This is hard waiting."

His mother put a hand on his arm, about as demonstrative a display of affection as she ever gave. "It was a hard wait to get that house for your kids, too. But you got it, and now you got only a little while longer until you got custody. You know how to wait."

"This seems so different."

"Why?"

He opened his mouth, then realized he didn't have a ready answer.

His mother patted his arm, then left him to think about it.

Chapter Twenty

San Diego was as warm and sunny as ever, and it didn't look a bit different from when she'd left in August, only three months ago. Shelley knew exactly how long it took to drive north from the airport to her parents' house in La Jolla, and she knew which camellia bushes would be blooming in her parents' front yard. It was hard to believe that she'd been away so short a time when it seemed as though a lifetime separated her from the life she'd led here. Could three months constitute a lifetime?

Her parents were happy to see her, but careful around her. They didn't ask her too many questions, and Shelley noticed on the ride home that they automatically made decisions for her.

"Mary Ann Adams had her baby," her father mentioned. Mary Ann was one of the women she had taught with. "I ran into her at the juice bar last week. I'll bet she'd love to hear from you."

Her mother frowned and shook her head. "Shelley's only going to be here a little while, Chase. She probably won't have time."

After listening to several similar exchanges in which neither of her parents appeared to expect any response from her, Shelley realized that she'd let her parents make most of her decisions during the years since Brad had been killed, right down to the inconsequential details of her social calendar. Actually, she had pretty well withdrawn from most social activities, so there hadn't been much to decide.

Shelley leaned forward in her seat. "Is Mary Ann's baby a boy or a girl?"

Her mother looked back in surprise.

"A boy. He's a big fella," her father supplied.

"Did she say how much he weighed?"

"Almost ten pounds. And he was twenty-two inches long."

"A monster baby," Shelley groaned. "I'll have to call her. That must have been some delivery for the first time around."

She didn't miss the speculative look that passed between her parents.

Later that evening, after a light dinner on the patio, Shelley pleaded an all too real exhaustion and escaped to her room. There, in the bottom corner of her closet, she unearthed a green wooden box that one of her grandfathers had made as a toy chest for her mother, decades in the past. Shelley had always used it to store her childhood treasures. Now it held things she had thought too awful to look at for over four long years, things she had kept only because the pain they caused was the only connection she had had to everything she had lost.

Heaving the box out into the room, Shelley lifted the

latch with trepidation. What would happen? Could she stand to do this? Should she wait until morning?

Tired as she was, she couldn't wait. With reverent care, she opened the box and began to lift out the contents.

First there were the photo albums from college. Then the wedding album, and then several books that recorded vacations and birthdays and other milestones. There was a stack of letters from the winter Brad had gone to Chicago on a fellowship.

Shelley looked through each album and read the letters, remembering the girl she'd been and then the young wife, and she remembered Brad. She cried a little, as she'd known she would, but she laughed, as well. She looked, and she remembered. Most of all, she felt, and what she felt wasn't all rage or helpless despair.

After more than an hour, only two items remained in the chest. Shelley lifted out a scrapbook, leaving the last item in the bottom of the box, and took a deep breath. This would be harder.

In the scrapbook were newspaper clippings about Brad's death and the subsequent trial. Her father had kept the macabre chronicle, saying that someday, she might want it. If she didn't, she never had to look at it, and she hadn't.

Tonight, she was glad she had it.

Starting at the beginning, Shelley read every article in the scrapbook. On occasion tears and fatigue blurred her vision, but she kept on.

It was nearly midnight when she was done, and Shelley felt drained, almost as if she had been through one of Verdell Owens's fifty-rock sweats. One last time, she reached into the box and picked up an envelope addressed to her in care of her attorney.

The letter inside consisted of two lined sheets torn

from a notebook, still crisp, barely handled. The handwriting was in blue pen, cramped and careful, a mixture of printing and cursive, with words crossed out and more than a few misspellings.

Shelley recalled the day she had received the letter. Her attorney had had it delivered, and she had been alone that summer afternoon. When the deliveryman left, she had opened it in the entryway and read it as she stood there. When she had finished, she had refolded it and slipped it back in the envelope, then dropped it into the trash.

Later, for reasons she hadn't understood at the time, she'd retrieved it and hidden it in the very bottom of this box. She had never planned to open it again.

Now it lay once more in her hand, and Shelley read it for the second time.

Blinking to clear her eyes of tears, Shelley experienced everything she'd felt during the past three months, all the anger, all the futility, all the sorrow. She let the feelings and the thoughts come as they would, and when the same deep, hiccuping sobs she'd cried in Blue's arms last night came again, she gave herself over to her grief.

When the tears finally stopped, Shelley still held Emilio's letter in her hand, and she knew that what he had done was wrong and would always be wrong. There was a part of her that would always hate what he had done, that might always hate him. But she had seen how desperation could push a young man or woman to terrible lengths. She had seen Bethany, a girl she had unwillingly cared about, pushed toward the worst possible options. Violence wore a human face for her now, and for the first time, she saw humanity when she saw Emilio Ossario's name neatly printed at the end of his letter.

Beneath his name, he had written the name and address of a prison counselor through whom he could be reached.

It took longer than Shelley had hoped to arrange the visit with Emilio at the state prison where he was housed, and she wasn't able to make her appointment until Wednesday. On Saturday afternoon, she called Blue to let him know she wouldn't be back Sunday, but he wasn't in. Knowing it was cowardly, she left a message, telling him she would call again later. Until she knew how she felt after seeing Emilio, she wasn't ready to decide whether she would go back.

At long last, she'd been able to articulate for herself that she had to let go of more than Brad in order to recover her heart and go on. The dream she'd had of Brad in the sky had helped. Now she had to find forgiveness for Emilio and the state of affairs that allowed terrible things to happen to good people. She wasn't sure she could forgive entirely, but she had to release much of the anger and grief in her heart.

Blue had showed her what she would be missing if she didn't. She wanted to be free enough of the past to meet him as a partner, not as some emotionally stunted leech who would soak up all his love without giving him the love he needed and deserved.

If she was going to live with Blue, she had to control the urge to hide away inside herself from everything that was ugly or difficult. Living with Blue meant sharing responsibilities for his children and that was not something she would undertake lightly. She didn't have to be completely strong all the time, but she had to be willing to engage more fully than she had been.

As every day passed, Shelley wanted her marriage to work more. It was becoming harder to imagine her life without Blue, and she knew that if she failed to move through this struggle, she would pay dearly for it. She continued to be frustrated with herself, for it shouldn't seem like such a difficult choice to make. Either grow and embrace the promise of love and joy her marriage offered, or accept a lesser life, one defined by failure and grief. Yet the rage she felt still frightened her. It had to be tempered before she could move on. She was close, she thought. Close enough to know that living without Blue would probably be more painful than living with him.

On Wednesday morning, she stood in the dismal visitors' waiting room at the Richard J. Donovan Correctional Facility. She supposed someone had thought the yellow paint cheery when it was new, but it was worn and dingy now, too bilious by far for a stomach as queasy as hers. The old inclination to hide was strong, but so was her need to know whether she could ever hope for the life she might have with Blue.

In the end, she wondered why she had been so frightened. Emilio Ossario, a small young man, had been embarrassed and ashamed, then contrite. He had cried a little, and so had she when she had thanked him for his letter and explained that it had taken her a long time to be able to respond. He had nodded sagely, with far more knowing in his dark eyes than such a young man should have, she thought.

He looked, she realized, a great deal like her Lakota students in South Dakota with his even brown skin and glossy black hair. He wasn't much older than they were.

He told her about his studies when she asked, stammering a time or two. It didn't take long before neither of them had anything left to say. Shelley rose to go.

"I am so sorry, Mrs. Mathews," he said again in softly accented English.

She nodded, acknowledging his guilt as he acknowledged her loss.

"All my life," he continued, speaking formally, as though he had rehearsed the words many times over, "I will bear the burdens of what I took from you in my heart. I've prayed that you would not bear such burdens for so long a time. I pray that you will find someone to love again, someone who will love you and be a family for you."

Shelley let his benediction wash over her, and she knew from the easy way the tears fell without strangling her throat, without harsh sobs or broken breath, that she had the answer to this boy's prayers within grasp.

All she had to do was take it.

When she woke up Thursday morning refreshed and eager for the day, she thought of Blue and did a quick inventory of her heart.

She missed him. His image sprang to mind with ease, and she felt her fingers itch to caress his face. Her arms felt empty without him there to fill them. Then she surveyed the warmth she felt. There was desire there, most certainly, and the deep appreciation for his generosity of spirit and his open heart.

And there was joy. She felt it as a bubble of laughter that brought her close to tears even as it spilled from her lips as a giggle. Holding it close, Shelley turned the joy around and examined it for flaws.

Closing her eyes, she pictured her heart. There were some tough areas here and there, like scar tissue lying in thickened ropes, but underneath each flaw, tender flesh throbbed and pulsed with life. She poked at things. There was fear in a few places, especially the fear that she might lose Blue. She didn't think she could make that go away, but neither was she so certain as she had been that the fear was strong enough to override the joy. Yes, a few places in her heart were still a little tough and there were still bruises there, but no longer did she feel anything that was rock hard and frozen.

Shelley rolled onto her stomach and buried her face in her pillow to catch the laughter she couldn't contain. She wasn't perfect. Those scars would give her trouble yet, no doubt. She would always miss Brad, and she would always be angry about the senseless violence that had taken his life.

But she was alive, gloriously and completely alive.

And she was in love—just as gloriously and completely in love with Blue Larson.

Leaping out of bed, she snagged her robe off a chair and sailed out the door.

"Mom! Dad! Are you up?"

She found them in the kitchen eating bagels and fruit.

"Are you feeling all right?" her mother asked cautiously.

Shelley beamed at them and dropped a kiss on each of their upturned faces. "I haven't been this all right in a very long time. I have some things to tell you about." She pulled out a chair and plopped down. "First of all, and I know this will come as something of a surprise, maybe a shock, but I got married again."

Shock was indeed an apt description of her parents' expressions.

"His name is Blue Larson. He's the man I told you was my roommate, but we were married in September. We got married initially more for convenience than anything else—"

Her mother gasped.

"I know, but just wait. He's the most wonderful man, and he's so good to me. We met when we both tried to rent the same house...."

Blue was fit to be tied. Shelley had called once while he'd been out, leaving a flustered-sounding message that only said she wouldn't be back on Sunday. He hadn't heard from her since, and he'd been trying like the blazes to take his mother's advice and wait patiently, but it was hell. He hadn't slept more than a few hours at a time since he got back from taking the kids to meet Carlene, and he was having a devil of a time concentrating. With final exams next week, the timing couldn't have been worse.

It was his heart that was in the worst shape, though. He was worried about Shelley. He wanted to do something. Anything but just sitting around waiting.

By Thursday evening, he felt like a zombie. He'd spread his finance texts all around him at the kitchen table in a futile attempt to study, but the words and figures blurred. His mind wandered. He wondered where she was, what she was doing. He wondered if she missed him a fraction of how much he missed her, and he wondered why she didn't call.

After two hours he gave up the pretense of studying, turned off all the lights and put some music on the stereo. Sitting in the dark, listening to a CD, he found it hard to believe that only a little more than a week passed since they had spent the night making love.

There was only one way she could have made love with him the way she had that night.

She loved him.

She just had to, and he just had to trust she'd figure that out—sometime in this lifetime.

Fantasies filled his head. He imagined flying out to San Diego like a knight in shining armor rescuing a fair maiden. When she saw him again, she would know her heart and run into his arms, proclaiming what a fool she'd been. He would carry her off along some California beach, the sun setting over the ocean, and they would make love through endless nights.

Or the phone would ring, and she would say, "I'm coming home," her voice thick with love and emotion. He would drive in to Rapid to pick her up, take her up to some romantic hideaway in the Black Hills and lose a week or two to love.

The daydreams made him ache for her body next to his, and all kinds of erotic images filled his fantasies. He had yet to see her in that sexy piece of fluff that had come from a lingerie catalog. He'd found it in the boxes in the bedroom when he'd ripped them open and put her things back in her drawers. Time enough to repack it all if she asked him to send it. In the meantime, he would cling to what he could.

Lost in a sleepy haze of yearning fantasy, he dozed and dreamed. In his dream, he heard her key in the lock, and the rattle of the glass. He heard Shoonk snuffle a greeting, and he thought he even smelled the vivid snap of winter in the cold draft that cut through the house when the door was opened.

He heard her voice calling him over the soft music, and it was so real, he frowned in his sleep at the tricks his mind could play on him. Her touch, her scent…it was all so real. He could even feel her tongue in his ear, and the chill of the night wind on her cheek against his neck.

"Wake up, sleepyhead," she whispered.

He refused to open his eyes and lose the fantasy.

Kisses covered his jaw. Then one eyelid was rudely pulled open.

"Blue?"

Through one unfocused eye, he thought he saw Shelley sitting astride his thigh.

"I thought I might get a more enthusiastic welcome," she complained as she made to rise.

Taking no chances, he made a grab for her. His hands filled with heavy wool and solid woman.

Dear God, it was really her.

He pulled her into his arms. "You came back." He didn't care if his voice shook.

She kissed him gently. "I did."

He held her away from him to look at her, to convince himself she was really there. Suddenly, he didn't know what to say, where to start.

Shelley reached for the lamp and flicked it on, then held his face in her hands as she waited for his eyes to adjust.

"I want to say this in the light. I love you, Blue." There was not a trace of sorrow in her eyes. "I'm ready to make this a real marriage. In every sense of the word. For as long as we both shall live."

His hands tightened at her waist, and his heart thudded. "You came back," he repeated.

She laughed at him. "Yes. I came home to you. I don't need to hide so much anymore. I don't want to hide from everything that matters most in life, and I'm tired of holding my anger and fears inside me as a shield to keep love out. I'm still afraid of losing you, but I love you, and I want to spend whatever time I might be granted in this lifetime with you."

He pulled her closer, or she pulled him—he couldn't

really tell. He only knew he had to get closer to her, get that wool coat out of the way, and kiss his wife again and again and again as they explored a love he knew would last forever.

Epilogue

The aspens in Spearfish Canyon captured the September
light and danced with it, sending golden disks spinning
high into the sky. One leaf fluttered gracefully down to
land on the notebook at Shelley's side. Another landed
on her prone husband's cheek, and he batted it away
without opening his eyes.

Shelley laughed, her voice clear and bright in the early
autumn air, a counterpoint to the low rush of water in the
creek beside their picnic site.

Blue smiled, then opened his eyes. "I love to hear you
laugh like that."

She laughed a lot these days. "Sit up." She tugged at
his arm, and he complied, then pulled her onto his lap.
Lightly, he nibbled at her neck, and she sighed, then
ducked out of reach. "In a minute. Let's update our
plan."

"The Plan with a capital *P*," Blue intoned with mock gravity.

Shelley giggled, then adopted the same tone. "Yes. The Plan with a capital *P*. This is our formal anniversary assessment. This is serious business. We have some things to check off this year."

It was their second wedding anniversary, and as they had last year, they'd returned to the Black Hills for a few days alone. On their first anniversary, they'd brought the notebook in which Shelley had written down her Plan with a capital *P*. She had composed it the day after she'd returned from California to tell Blue she intended to stay and make their marriage a real one. A year ago in September, while on a picnic in the canyon, they had formally checked off the goals they had written down the winter before, and decided to make an annual event of it.

Shelley looked at last year's check by the part of the plan that called for gaining joint custody of Libby and Travis. Blue's children had moved in with them a little more than a year ago.

"On the whole, I think it's been a successful year," she announced. "Libby and Travis are both doing better in school, and I think they're doing well all around."

"And Libby's settled down a lot," Blue added.

Shelley suppressed a grin. "After a few trials, yes. Like the time she hitchhiked to Lodgepole to visit her cousins and stayed out all night."

Blue grimaced. "And the time she got mad and took Jewel out without asking and it started to snow. Hard."

"And the day in Sioux Falls at the mall," Shelley reminded him.

They groaned in unison remembering the scene Libby

had caused when they had tried to separate her from a boy she'd met. Then they laughed.

"I'm glad you can laugh about it." Blue kissed her temple. "She hasn't always been too nice to you this past year."

"She's a teenager, and I'm her stepmother. Things have certainly gone better than I expected them to." She looked into his coffee dark eyes. "Everything's gone better than I expected."

"For me, too." His lips lifted in a smile, and she had a hard time looking away.

"Let's look at that plan," he said, taking the notebook. "Looks like this year some of these things we can check off were parts of my plan from way back."

Shelley put her pen in his hand. "Then I think you should mark them off."

"They would never have happened without you." He placed her hand over his. "Let's check it together."

"Okay. Which one first?"

"Make the down payment on our own place." Once again laughter bubbled up from inside both of them, and they made the check with a flourish. Mr. Heber had agreed to sell them the house and two sections at a very good price. They had made the down payment and taken out a mortgage in April.

"The old man mended his ways," Shelley said.

"Maybe. Or maybe he couldn't say no to the prettiest tenant he ever had."

"It was more than that. He knew he made a mistake when he refused to rent to you, and when he saw how you were taking care of things, I think he was ashamed of himself."

Blue ran a thumb over her cheek. "My mom says once

at senior citizens bingo she heard him take credit for introducing us."

Shelley shook her head. "I guess if he hadn't been so difficult, we might not be here today."

"Yes, we would have. I'd have found you and snapped you right up wherever you lived." He took a small bite of her neck.

"Okay, don't start that yet." She squirmed away from him and the delightfully wicked sensation he provoked. "We aren't done with the plan."

"Next check, then."

"The next check is for your business." Together with one of his friends who was a CPA, Blue had started a small business serving the financial and accounting needs of local businesses. They'd had a solid first year, and were expanding at a steady rate.

Hand in hand, they made the check.

"Now, what are we checking off for you?" Blue asked, lips brushing warm across her ear.

"Well, there's one thing I can't check off yet but I'd like to aim for next year."

"What's that?"

She pointed to an entry in the middle of the page.

Blue grew suddenly still. "Are you sure?"

She nodded. "We should probably talk to Libby and Travis about it, but that's what I want."

Dropping the pen they held, Blue turned her face to his and gave her a kiss as slow and sweet as the first one he'd given her over two years ago. "We don't need to talk to the kids," he said when he finally broke the kiss. "Last weekend Libby asked me what was taking us so long to have a baby. She thinks it would be nice to have a new brother or sister. Travis prefers a brother, in case we're taking orders. So there's no need to wait. We can get to work on that one right away." He closed one hand over her breast and squeezed.

She slapped his hand away. "Maybe we should wait until we're back at the hotel."

He flipped her onto her back and pinned her beneath him, settling between her legs. "Maybe we shouldn't."

"Wait," she said, before he could kiss her again. "I have one more thing to check off."

"What now?" Blue growled.

Shelley pushed until she managed to roll them both onto their sides. "Here." She pointed to the last entry.

"Be happy," it read.

"You checked that one last year," Blue said, nuzzling her jaw.

"I'm going to check it every year." She solemnly took the pen and fitted her hand under his. Together they made the last check. "It still feels like a miracle, Blue. I think it always will."

"You've earned a miracle or two, I'd say."

She thought back to her wedding day two years before with the same humility and sense of blessing Blue's love so often inspired in her. "You brought me back to life."

"You brought me love." This time, when he rolled her over onto her back and kissed her, she didn't protest. Instead she wrapped her arms tight around him and kissed him back.

Under the blue sky, with golden leaves shimmering all around them in the air, they celebrated the miracles they brought to one another with joy and abiding peace.

* * * * *

Take 2 bestselling love stories FREE

Plus get a FREE surprise gift!

Special Limited-Time Offer

Mail to Silhouette Reader Service™

3010 Walden Avenue
P.O. Box 1867
Buffalo, N.Y. 14240-1867

YES! Please send me 2 free Silhouette Special Edition® novels and my free surprise gift. Then send me 6 brand-new novels every month, which I will receive months before they appear in bookstores. Bill me at the low price of $3.57 each plus 25¢ delivery and applicable sales tax, if any.* That's the complete price, and a saving of over 10% off the cover prices—quite a bargain! I understand that accepting the books and gift places me under no obligation ever to buy any books. I can always return a shipment and cancel at any time. Even if I never buy another book from Silhouette, the 2 free books and the surprise gift are mine to keep forever.

235 SEN CH7W

Name	(PLEASE PRINT)	
Address		Apt. No.
City	State	Zip

This offer is limited to one order per household and not valid to present Silhouette Special Edition® subscribers. *Terms and prices are subject to change without notice. Sales tax applicable in N.Y.

USPED-98

©1990 Harlequin Enterprises Limited

We, the undersigned, having barely survived four years of nursing school, do hereby vow to meet at Granetti's at least once a week, not to do anything drastic to our hair without consulting each other first and never, _ever_—no matter how rich, how cute, how funny, how smart, or how good in bed—marry a doctor.

Dana Rowan, R.N.
Lee Murphy, R.N.
Katie Sheppard, R.N.

Christine Flynn
Susan Mallery
Christine Rimmer

prescribe a massive dose of heart-stopping romance in their scintillating new series, **PRESCRIPTION: MARRIAGE**. Three nurses are determined _not_ to wed doctors— only to discover the men of their dreams come with a medical degree!

Look for this unforgettable series in fall 1998:

October 1998: **FROM HOUSE CALLS TO HUSBAND** by Christine Flynn

November 1998: **PRINCE CHARMING, M.D.** by Susan Mallery

December 1998: **DR. DEVASTATING** by Christine Rimmer

Only from

Silhouette®SPECIAL EDITION®

Available at your favorite retail outlet.

COMING NEXT MONTH

#1207 A FAMILY KIND OF GAL—Lisa Jackson
That Special Woman!
Forever Family
All Tiffany Santini wanted was a life of harmony away from her
domineering in-laws. But a long-ago attraction was reignited when her
sinfully sexy brother in-law, J.D., decided this single mom needn't raise her
kids all alone. Could he tempt Tiffany to surrender all her love—to him?

**#1208 THE COWGIRL & THE UNEXPECTED WEDDING—
Sherryl Woods**
And Baby Makes Three: The Next Generation
Once, headstrong Lizzy Adams had captured Hank Robbins's heart, but
he'd reluctantly let her go. Now they were together again, and their pent-up
passion couldn't be denied. What would it take for a fit-to-be-tied cowboy
to convince a mule-headed mother-to-be to march down the aisle?

#1209 PRINCE CHARMING, M.D.—Susan Mallery
Prescription: Marriage
Just about every nurse at Honeygrove Memorial Hospital was swooning
shamelessly over debonair doc Trevor MacAllister. All except disillusioned
Dana Rowan, who vowed to never, ever wed a doctor—much less be lured
by Trevor's Prince Charming act again. But *some* fairy tales are destined to
come true....

#1210 UNTIL YOU—Janis Reams Hudson
Timid Anna Collins knew what to expect from her quiet, predictable life.
Until she discovered a sexy stranger sleeping on her sofa. Suddenly her
uninvited houseguest made it his mission to teach her about all of life's
pleasures. Would he stick around for the part about when a man loves a
woman?

#1211 A MOTHER FOR JEFFREY—Trisha Alexander
Leslie Marlowe was doing a good job of convincing herself that she wasn't
meant to be anyone's wife—or mother. But then young Jeffrey Canfield
came into her life, followed by his strong, sensitive father, Brian. Now the
only thing Leslie had to convince herself of was that she wasn't dreaming!

#1212 THE RANCHER AND THE REDHEAD—Allison Leigh
Men of the Double-C Ranch
Matthew Clay was set in his ways—and proud of it, too. So when virginal
city gal Jaimie Greene turned his well-ordered ranch into Calamity Central,
the sassy redhead had him seething with anger and consumed with desire.
Dare he open his home—and his heart—to the very *last* woman he
should love?